Convoluted Tales

2.0

J.P. Johnson

Lost Lake Folk Art
SHIPWRECKT BOOKS PUBLISHING COMPANY

IN®
DIE

Rushford, Minnesota

Front cover photo adapted from original NOAA Photo
Library, NOAA Central Library; OAR/ERL/National
Severe Storms Laboratory (NSSL), Cordell, Oklahoma,
May 22, 1981

Cover, graphic & interior design by Shipwreckt Books.

For their encouragement to use my imagination to its fullest, I dedicate this story collection to my mother and my brother.

Convoluted Tales 2.0

Quiz Show

My family finally got a TV when I was about twelve. Funny thing though, my parents rarely watched it. Among my favorites was, *Masquerade Party*. There'd be celebrities who'd wear heavy, latex masks and a panel of lesser celebrities would try to guess who it was. In my opinion, the best part of the show was when the mystery guests unmasked themselves. They would peel off the latex (it looked rather painful) and the panelists and audience would gasp and cheer.

I also liked *To Tell the Truth* and *Play Your Hunch*. But, the show I absolutely hated was, *What's My Secret?* I think it was broadcast live from New York. Thanks to cable TV and *Buzzr*, I'm now able to re-watch some of those shows. Even, What's My Secret?

The episode I remember from when I was a kid was the appearance of Dick Beemer, middle linebacker for the *Monsters of the Midway*, Chicago Bears. Beemer was wearing fake, horn-rimmed glasses, presumably as a disguise, and dressed in a business suit. The foursome panel, woman, man, woman, man were East Coast intellectuals, or so they thought. The host wrote a newspaper column as did two members of the panel, although they probably made more money from television. One of the panelists, Christopher Bennet, was also a book publisher and editor, who had dozens of writers under contract. He did no editing himself. His staff would routinely reject manuscripts usually based on the first sentence. Bennet knew a lot of celebrities whom he entertained in his penthouse suite. As a result, he'd oftentimes guess who the mystery guest was.

Beemer wasn't a mystery guest. *I* knew who he was and so did the audience as soon as he signed in with a piece of chalk on the blackboard. The panel, then, tried to guess his profession.

The first question was asked by some-time stage and TV actress with the preposterous name of Frances Drake, who always asked the obligatory question: "Are you in show business?" She was looking directly at this huge, rough-hewn man. He scowled back at her and said, "No."

The next question was offered by a has-been Borsht Belt comic who did frequent stand-up comedy at Grossinger's Resort: "Are you a comedy writer?" Again, "No." On to a woman columnist, Dorothy Donahue, whose close friends, all five of them, called her, Dee Dee. "Are you someone who works with his hands?" After the host consulted with him, Beemer answered, "Yes." Now, it was the main egghead's turn, Christopher Bennet: "You can't be a business man because you look much too brutish. What are you, a writer? Your fingers are too large to use a typewriter. A professional wrestler? Are you a football player?"

"Yes he is," the host announced, cheerfully and both he and Beemer stood. The host offered his hand. Beemer refused to shake it and instead chose to stalk toward Bennet. Bennet stood and held out his hand. Beemer took it, told him that he was a sniveling punk and proceeded to crush Bennet's hand, bringing him to his knees, yelping in pain, "I think you broke it!" The other panelists quickly withdrew from the stage. Then, Beemer shouted at the host and audience that he was in town for Sunday's game with the Giants and promised that he'd put one, or two Giants' players in the hospital. He threw the fake glasses at the host.

This is exactly how I remember it. Buzzr, however, cut out what I thought was the best part, making room for vintage commercials as well as new ones.

This happened back in 1959. Eisenhower was President and all seemed to be well except for tenuous relations with the Soviets, but old Ike could handle them. In the few years which followed, our nation would begin unravelling. Just about everyone thought World War Three was inevitable. Some paranoids started digging fallout shelters. I, on the other hand, hoped the Russians would drop a bomb on my Junior High School.

No Nose Is Bad News

"**F**rankie!" his mother called, "do you want to spend the weekend at your grandpa's?"

"Yes!" Frankie answered in an excited voice. Frankie never passed up a chance to be with Grandpa. He thought his grandpa was not only the coolest guy in the world, but he was also a great, professional magician who knew lots of cool tricks.

Frankie rushed around the house, gathering things to bring with him. He found the trick coin that his grandpa gave him and thought he would take it along to show Grandpa how he had practiced that trick to perfection.

"Mom, where's the trick glasses Grandpa gave me?"

"They're probably in your dresser drawer. What are those glasses for, again?"

"They're for seeing the backs of playing cards that are marked with invisible ink."

"I'll have to speak to Grandpa about that," his mother said, sternly. He shouldn't be teaching you card tricks like that."

"But, Mom ..." Frankie's words trailed off.

"Are you going to be ready to go when your dad comes home, so he can give you a ride to Grandpa's?"

"Sure, I'll be ready, Mom." Frankie slipped the trick glasses that he found in his dresser, into his backpack.

Frankie ran to greet his dad as soon as he came in through the door, giving him a big hug.

"Hold on there, champ!" Frankie's dad said. "What's all the excitement about?"

Mom answered, "Frankie wants to go to Grandpa's house. Can you give him a ride? I'll keep your dinner warming in the oven 'til you get home."

It took about forty-five minutes to drive to Grandpa's house, but Frankie's dad didn't mind very much because he thought Grandpa was pretty cool, too and that magic tricks were fun for a boy to learn.

"Have a good time!" Frankie's mom called, waving from the front door, as she watched the car back out of the driveway.

The car turned off the main highway and onto a narrow, dirt road which led into the woods and Grandpa's house. It was Fall and the car made a swooshing sound as it rolled over the thick blanket of dried leaves covering the road.

Grandpa's house was a small, cozy, comfortable-looking cottage, nestled among tall oak and pine trees. There was a plume of white smoke coming from his fireplace chimney. Frankie saw his grandpa waiting on his front porch, as they approached.

"Hi, you guys!" Grandpa shouted, cheerfully, as he shuffled through the leaves.

Frankie's grandpa was a tall, thin man with a thick mane of white hair, white goatee and mustache.

"He looks exactly like a magician should look." Frankie told his dad, who smiled and nodded, as Frankie got out of the car.

"Now you behave, Frankie and do what your grandpa tells you," his dad said.

"He always does," Grandpa replied, "he's a good boy."

Grandpa slung an arm around Frankie's shoulder. "You know what? I think your dad worries too much."

They stood and watched Frankie's dad drive away, as leaves swirled behind the car.

"Hey Grandpa, before we go inside, could you do the 'I got your nose, trick?' That's one of my favorites." Even though Frankie was ten-years-old, he never got tired of his grandpa doing that trick and it made both of them laugh.

"Okay, Frankie. I hope I remember how to do it," he joked.

Just then, Frankie looked up at the sky. "Grandpa, look at that huge crow flying around."

"Oh, that's that pesky Jimmy the Crow. He's always hanging around, bothering me with his annoying voice. Do you want me to do the nose trick, now?"

"Sure."

Grandpa placed his fingers on each side of Frankie's nose and pulled. "Oh, my goodness!" Grandpa shouted, "I forgot how to do it!" Frankie's nose went sailing into a pile of leaves.

Frankie touched the spot where his nose used to be. "Grandpa, my nose ..."

4

"Don't worry, Frankie. I'll get it and put it back on."

Suddenly, Jimmy the Crow swooped down onto the leaves, snatched Frankie's nose and flew away.

"Now, how am I supposed to wear those trick glasses?" cried Frankie, "they'll fall right off my face!"

"Hurry," Grandpa said, as he nudged Frankie toward the door, "I've got a plan."

"What plan, Grandpa?" Frankie asked, trying to hold back tears.

"We're going to give Jimmy the Crow a run for his money," Grandpa explained.

"What does that mean?"

"It means that we're going to try to beat Jimmy the Crow to the *Kingdom of No Noses*. First, I have to phone Tony the Taxi-driver."

"The Kingdom of No Noses? And a taxi's going to take us there?" Frankie asked, his head was filled with questions.

"Yes, Frankie," said Grandpa, with the most serious tone that Frankie's ever heard from his grandpa, "it's a magic taxi and it's going to bring us to where Jimmy the Crow flew off with your nose."

"How many miles away is it?"

"It's not exactly measured in miles because where we're going is a magical place where distance doesn't mean anything." Frankie's mouth dropped open at his grandpa's explanation. Grandpa noticed Frankie's confused expression and added, with an agitated tone, "Hey, that's the best explanation I can give. After all, I'm a magician, not a scientist."

Grandpa picked up the phone and mumbled something that Frankie couldn't quite hear. "How can a taxi beat Jimmy the Crow to the Kingdom of No Noses?" asked Frankie. As soon as he said it, they both heard a car horn blowing outside in the driveway.

"There's no time to waste, Frankie. The taxi's here. Let's go. You can leave your backpack and the rest of your stuff, here. We'll be back, soon."

Tony, the driver bounded out of the shiny, yellow taxi and opened the back door. "Hi, Max! and you must be Frankie. Your grandpa's told me a lot about you." It was unusual for Frankie to hear Grandpa's real name. He never thought of his grandpa as, Max.

"Cut the chatter, Tony and step on it!" Grandpa said, seriously.

"Yes sir."

Grandpa turned to Frankie and said, reassuringly, "I got you into this and I'll get you out of this."

Frankie nodded and then looked out the window and saw that everything was going by in a blur. Then, he leaned forward, from his place in the backseat and looked at the taxi's speedometer. "Holy cow!" Frankie yelled, this thing's going five-hundred miles an hour!"

"Sure," Grandpa laughed, "I told Tony to 'step on it' and he did."

"Are we flying, Grandpa? I think we just passed a cloud!"

"Yes, it's the only way to beat traffic."

Tony looked at Frankie's nose, or where it used to be, then at Grandpa in the rearview mirror, laughed and asked, "Say Max, did you forget how to do the 'got your nose' trick?"

Grandpa smiled and said, "Never mind. Just keep driving."

"Frankie," Tony said, "did you know that Max, I mean, your grandpa, is one of the most famous magicians in the world?"

"Really?" Frankie sounded surprised and stared at his grandpa.

"Yes," Tony answered, "He's known from Zanzibar to Cleveland."

Frankie heard Grandpa chuckling and wondered why.

The taxi finally glided to a stop outside of a large, stone gate. "This is it," Grandpa said. "We'll have to walk from here. Tony, we won't be long, so you can wait. Let's go, Frankie."

On the arch above the gate, were the words: "The Kingdom of No Noses." Inside the gate, Grandpa and Frankie saw people of all sizes and shapes, young and old. Some with noses and some without. Grandpa said, as he looked around, "Making plastic noses is their main industry, here."

"How come some people have noses and some don't?"

Grandpa stroked his goatee and said, "You see, Frankie, all the people of this kingdom were born without noses, so they either have to buy plastic noses or, get real noses from Jimmy the Crow, who steals them."

"How much do the plastic noses cost?"

"Oh, I hear that they're very expensive," Grandpa answered, still looking around at people walking by. "Some people are so poor, they can't afford fake noses."

6

"So, only rich people have noses?" Before his grandpa could answer, he asked another question: "Why don't they just give poor people noses? They need them as much as rich people."

"Well, sometimes that's not the way it works … "

Frankie interrupted, "Look at that little girl! I think she's got my nose!"

"Are you sure? You've got to be sure."

"Yes, look at all the freckles and I've got exactly the same freckles!"

Frankie started running toward the girl and Grandpa had to hold him back. "Wait a minute, Frankie, you'd better let me handle this." Frankie watched him approach the girl. "Hi, little girl."

"How dare you address me in that manner! I'm not just any little girl, I'm a princess!"

"I'm so sorry, Your Highness, but I was wondering where people buy noses. I need one for my grandson. He's standing over there."

The girl didn't bother looking at Frankie. She turned and pointed to her left, "Over there."

When she turned, Grandpa grabbed her nose and pulled. It came off and Grandpa laughed, "Got your nose," and ran away. He put the nose in his pocket, grabbed Frankie's hand and they ran toward the taxi. Frankie was amazed at how fast his grandpa ran. Tony jumped into his taxi and started the engine.

The princess was in shock, putting her hands up, feeling around the place where the nose had been. "Guards, guards!" she screamed, as she whirled around in circles. Guards came running with their swords held high. But, it was too late. The taxi was already flying away.

Frankie asked his grandpa, "How are you going to put my nose back on?"

"I can't blame you for asking. You know what? I'm going to put your nose back on, right now. Tony, look in the rearview mirror and watch this. No one's ever seen me do the nose trick in reverse. Presto!" he said, with a wave of his hand. "You've got your nose back."

Frankie, Grandpa and Tony all laughed, as the taxi flew toward Grandpa's house.

"I can't wait to tell my mom and dad about our adventure!" Frankie shouted.

"No, Frankie, I don't think that's a good idea. Maybe we should keep this our own little secret for a while."

Give 'Em What They Want

Finally, at the age of fifty-two, I decided to quit my job as an accountant. CPA was my title. I felt that I was getting round-shouldered, my hips were widening and getting arthritic from doing nothing but sitting every day. So, I decided to try stand-up comedy. My co-workers thought I was funny. My wife didn't.

I remember telling her (in retrospect, I shouldn't have) that a life-long dream of mine was to do something in connection with show business. I regret pronouncing it, "biz." Newly married, we had our first fight. Not physical, of course. There was a lot of anger directed at me. It was something about the ridiculous implausibility of my plan. During her tirade, I remained outwardly stoic, but inwardly felt my own flush of anger quickly rising. I did something that I often did, after any subsequent altercation with her and that was to get in my car and mindlessly drive. That first time, I drove two-hundred miles south and back; coming home at 4 a.m., finding her sleeping and sidling into bed without waking her.

The last time I mentioned my dream was apparently the final straw for my wife, Amanda. After thirty years of marriage, divorce, followed separation. All of it was amicable. Our children, a boy and a girl were in their late teens when they moved out and went to college on two different coasts, found spouses and stayed there. No, they hadn't yet blessed us with grandkids.

"You can't do an entire act based on a few one-liners, Pete," she huffed. "Do you still think you can do this?"

I moved into a one-bedroom apartment downtown, shortly before we sold the house.

Comedy clubs seemed to be a burgeoning business. I phoned an agent, a Mr. Burns, went over to his office and did part of my act in person. He only chuckled, no belly-laughs.

"I guess you're good enough, Pete. I'll take twenty percent. That's standard these days," he said, while picking at a scab on his chin.

He got me some jobs right away and it was enough to pay the rent. But then, he actually had a brilliant idea: Appearing on local TV commercials. I called my ex-wife with that bit of news.

Amanda had nothing to say. She watched a lot of TV. So, whether she wanted to or not, she might get a glimpse of me.

Burns told me I'd have to audition for the pitchman position. I knew I could nail it.

I failed. Standing there, in front of a green screen and teleprompter, I heard the director say, "We'll call you ... next? Who's next?"

It was back to the clubs, some of which were nothing more than padded sewers in a basement where the main sport was getting drunk and heckling standup comics.

I was doing my act which consisted of stealing bits from long-dead comics. This gag was stolen from *recently* deceased Jerry Lewis, a poem: "Mary had a little watch, she swallowed it one day. / The doctor gave her castor oil, to pass the time away. The castor didn't work, the time it didn't pass. / So, if you wanna know what time it is ... lookup Mary's ... uncle. He's got a watch, too."

A woman in the front row, began heckling. I responded by telling her, "Please, ma'am, keep your knees together, I don't need to see that." Unfortunately, it started the entire crowd heckling me.

After explaining to my agent what had happened and why I was fired, I watched a florid flush rising from his neck, to his jowls, to his cheeks, then to his bald pate. His glasses began to steam up.

His voice, high-pitched at first, found the octave he wanted and nearly shouted, "Don't you realize that when they fired you, they fired me too? I'll just have to find you someplace where they don't know you. These club owners talk to each other."

There he was, depending on *me* so *he* could make a living as he was doing with his other clients. I could plainly see that. The greedy sonuvabitch. Did I have any reason to fire *him*? Perhaps, not yet.

"Yeah, you do the clubs and look at the audience. If they're younger, you can tell forty-year-old jokes. Sometimes, the audience ain't hip enough to tell political jokes, but who knows ... these days, anything goes, even jokes about the Pope. Just give 'em what they want."

"And what do they want?"

"How the hell should *I* know? I think that after a while, you'll learn to gauge those things."

And so, I went about touring the nightspots. I was making pretty good money. Actually, not as much as an accountant, but I was happier … was I? Amanda told me not to quit my job. It was a stable, steady income. This kind of work wasn't. Sometimes, I wish that I'd listened to her. If I had, I might still be with her. Then, I *would've* been happier.

Give 'em what they want? Could Burns be any less *ambiguous? And he calls himself a manager.*

I was signed up to work that night when I got a call from the Mower County Medical Examiner. "I had a hard time finding you, Mr. Walker. Are you related to Amanda Olson?"

Of course, she went back to using her maiden name. "Yes, she's … was my wife. We're divorced."

"Mr. Walker, I hate to tell you this, but she was involved in a serious car crash. I'm afraid she didn't survive … passed away at the scene."

I couldn't say anything and ended the call. I had thoughts, memories, both pleasant and terrible. I had all afternoon to drive … let the news sink in like a lead brick in my gut and took to the freeway. There was a lot of traffic. Not as much as rush hour, but still quite a lot more than I'd expected.

I drove, staying in the right lane. Up in front, in the left lane, was a big, white Lincoln with its right blinker flashing. It also had handicap plates. *Handicap plates on a brand-new Lincoln. Must've been from an insurance settlement.*

I didn't dare speed up, fearing the Lincoln would turn into my lane. This went on for about ten miles. Cars behind me were honking. They didn't want to be behind the Lincoln, or me. I sped up anyway just to see inside that car. Apparently, they were having an argument. An older woman was giving holy hell to the old guy who was driving. It was a one-sided argument. She was in there waving her arms around. I slowed down a bit and dropped back, giving them enough leeway. I didn't trust them. Cars honked.

What happened next is what I'd fully expected. The Lincoln started cutting right in front of me as we approached an exit.

I, Jerry Walker would give 'em what they want. Vision blurred by tears, I pushed the gas pedal to the floor.

A Night at the Office

O n the night of September 20th, 1982, a homicide was committed, the first in Pine City, Pine County, Minnesota in over forty years. It had shaken the community of 4,000, even after the perpetrator was caught and convicted.

Upon discovering the dead body of one of his agents, the owner and broker of Stone Ridge Realty, Mr. Neal Evans, phoned the Pine City P.D. Two squads were dispatched. He then called each of his thirteen remaining agents and told them an emergency meeting, attendance mandatory, will begin at 9:00 a.m. sharp. His message, vaguely ominous.

Four uniformed police officers milled around the crime scene while Evans stood in the doorway of his office waiting for his agents to arrive. The next police agencies to arrive were three forensic specialists, wearing white lab coats, along with two detectives from Pine County's Special Investigations Unit; Lieutenant Sharon Riley and Sergeant Steve Lupinski. The detectives thanked the local police, dismissed them and told them to go about their usual duties.

"One of you, I don't care who, can stay behind. Get a chair and sit by the front door and don't let anyone in." Lt. Riley said. To Evans: "I see that your agents are beginning to arrive.

"I don't want any of your people in here 'til the Medical Examiner leaves with the victim."

One of the forensic men spoke up, "Looks like this guy never saw it coming. Pretty grisly, if you ask me. Poor bastard got hit on the top of his head by a brick, at least four times!"

"Did you find any prints?" asked Sgt. Lupinski.

"No, the perp musta worn gloves, maybe cloth. There're a few bloody smears ... hey, here's something interesting." He bent down and picked up a large blue button with a gloved hand.

"Looks like it came off of a coat. It *was* raining pretty hard last night—probably a raincoat," the Lt. said and looked out the window, "it's *still* coming down, a little lighter now."

Sgt. Lupinski knelt down by the black exit door at the back of the office. "Lt., there's a wet spot on the carpet next to the door."

"Oh, that's easy, Steve. The killer took off his shoes. Why don't you open the door and see if there's a keyhole on the outside."

"Nope. Don't see any, but there's a doorbell for deliveries and a spotlight above the door."

"Stand away everybody. Gotta get some pictures," the crime scene photographer said.

"Look at that guy's bald head, Sharon. You can see that it was the edge of the brick and the force of the blows that did the most damage; actually crushed his skull. Some of the wounds look an inch deep."

"Steve, while we're waiting for the M.E. to get here, I think we should talk to Evans in his office."

Lt. Sharon Riley turned to the forensic man who found the blue button, "Are you gonna need that button?"

"No, I don't think so. There wouldn't be any good prints. If there are, they'd be unidentifiable partials."

Looks like the button was torn off. There's some thread still on it. She dropped it into a side pocket of her purse.

Evans pointed toward a hall tree. "You can hang your raincoats over there. Come in and sit down." Evans sank into a black, faux leather swivel chair behind a modest-sized desk. Above the desk were framed documents pertaining to business achievements as well as laudatory certificates and letters from local officials. No college diplomas, however.

Riley and Lupinski wore their badges; hers on a lanyard around her neck and his, clipped to his suit jacket breast pocket.

Evans laced his fingers behind his head revealing yellow, armpit stains on his white shirt. When he noticed that *they* noticed the stains, he leaned forward and put his elbows on the desk.

"I'm Lt. Sharon Riley and this is my partner, Sgt. Steve Lupinski. We're from the county's Special Investigations Unit and we're here to investigate this homicide."

Riley looked attractive in a tailored, gray, pinstriped pantsuit. Her dark, brown hair was tightly pulled into a ponytail. In contrast, Lupinski's black suit was rumpled and had that lived-in, possibly slept-in look. Lupinski was about ten years Riley's junior, but together, they looked similar in age.

Evans studied Riley: "I've always liked to see women advancing themselves, especially in police work."

"I've worked hard to get where I am and coming from a man such as yourself. I appreciate the flattery. Things are happening faster now." *I've come a long way, baby!*

Leveling her eyes at Evans: "Could we get down to the business at hand? What can you tell me about the victim?" she looked at a business card, "Harold Spencer. I'm not asking you if he had any enemies. I know that he had at least one."

Evans picked up a pen, ready to write on a notepad for names that wouldn't be forthcoming. "I know it's kinda early, but do you have any suspects?"

"At this point," Lupinski said, "no, not really."

Lupinski ran his fingers through unkempt blond hair.

Evans: "Well, I certainly didn't do it. Why would I want to kill my biggest producer?"

Riley: "No, I don't think you would."

Evans sat back in his chair, momentarily relieved.

"Tell me, Mr. Evans, what did you notice before discovering the victim?"

"I unlocked the door at about 7:45 this morning. When I come in that early, I usually watch TV," motioning toward a small TV sitting on the corner of a credenza across the room. "This morning, something was different, the lights were left on. I could see through the blinds. The last person to leave the office, is supposed to shut the lights off.

"I came in and saw Harold sprawled across his desk and all that *blood!* It was horrible. I didn't want a closer look, so I went right into my office and called the police."

It was Lupinski's turn: "The murder weapon was a brick, which was taken in as evidence. Can you tell me why someone wrote 'Betsy' on it?"

"That was a joke. You know, Betsy Brick."

"And can you tell me what it was used for?"

"A doorstop. We use it to prop open the back door. The janitor uses it to empty the trash and my agents who smoked, use that door and stand at the back of the building. I don't allow them to smoke in the office, or out in front."

Lt. Riley: "Did Mr. Spencer smoke?"

"Yes. When a group of them went out, Harold would walk to the end of the building. I think he wanted to be alone, for some reason."

"Was that his own desk? I mean, where he was found?"

"Yes. See how the rows of desks are set up? The waist-high cubicles are what separates them. And, I think no one wanted to be more separated from everyone than Harold. For a salesman, he was pretty anti-social. Nobody liked him, anyway. They were always complaining about him."

"What did they say about him?"

"They were always telling me that he was stealing their leads."

"How would he steal leads?"

"I don't know. I guess he would look in their mailboxes at the front desk."

"Would he have had the opportunity to do it?"

"Now that I think of it, he had the perfect opportunity. He offered to pull floor duty after hours and on weekends. That was a big help to me, since most agents try to avoid it."

Evans went on to explain floor duty. Whomever had that duty, would either sit at the front desk, or their own and take phone calls.

Riley laughed sardonically, "That's *why* he was your biggest producer! Didn't that occur to you?"

Harold Spencer did indeed, have amazing credentials. When he came over to Stone Ridge Realty six months earlier from another firm, he was their number one producer with over a million in sales. Neal Evans was grateful, no, anxious to sign the transfer papers ... no questions asked.

In his first two weeks at Stone Ridge, he had two sales and two more later that month. Evans, in his long career, had never thought it was possible. He had found his superstar in Harold Spencer.

"The new townhouse development, you might have seen it as you drove in—Harold sold four units! So, let the other agents grumble about him. I'm sure they're just envious."

Lupinski to Evans: "Could be, Mr. Evans. I'm curious about his relationship with his co-workers."

"He didn't interact with anyone. Not at all. He was a lone wolf, so-to-speak. If there was an office party at a bar or restaurant, he wouldn't attend. Instead, he would be in the office. One time, I chartered a bus, bought tickets for all my agents and went to a Twins game at the Dome. He didn't want to be with us. I guess he *was* sort of strange."

"Other than that," the Lt. chimed in, "what did he say to you about his co-workers?"

"He thought they were stealing *his* leads, which I found utterly ridiculous. They're a good group. They wouldn't do that."

"Simply put, it's called, transference." She gave a subtle eye roll to her partner. "I understand, Mr. Evans, that you have sales meetings every Tuesday morning followed by a tour of new listings. Is that right?"

"Yes."

"Did Mr. Spencer participate?"

"He did, but he said things during the meeting that were disruptive."

"Like what?'

"Oh, like how we *should* do business. He said nothing new, nothing innovative. Speaking of the tours, Harold always drove by himself, while the others took turns car-pooling. Then, he'd go right home."

"Would he come back to the office later that night?"

"No, not on Tuesday or, Thursday nights because that's when the janitor came in. That might've distracted him."

"We're going to have to notify his family," Sgt. Lupinski said, "did he live alone? Did he have any relatives in this area or anywhere else?"

"He lived alone. That's all I know."

"Harold, if you care, I'm leaving now. Be sure to lock the front door."

Harold grunted a response without looking up from papers on his desk.

Get fucked, Harold! It used to be pleasant working here 'til you came. Now, it's so toxic! Think I'll go home for a while and check on my daughter.

She works hard at school. I wonder if she could use a break. Shit, it's still raining!

"Hi, Barb. Do you want to go out and have a drink with me?"

"I can't. I've got to study for a test tomorrow. It's a tough one. Maybe some other time, okay?"

"All right, I'll go by myself. Don't wait up."

"And don't you *drink* too much."

Don't worry. It'll only take just one.

Betsy Brick was in place, propping open the back door. Even when Spencer was alone, he went out in back to smoke.

A thin track of asphalt allowed the garbage truck access to the dumpster, but it had to back up a half-block from the street.

In a few moments, a murder was going to happen. A clear voice, a *command hallucination* rang in the killer's brain. *Take the brick away from the door. Don't let it slam shut. Remove your wet shoes. The son of a bitch took the folder off of your desk. He doesn't know they're fake listings. He's paging through the reverse directory. He's on the phone and doesn't hear you. As soon as he hangs up ... Do it, do it now!*

Raising the brick overhead, the killer brought the brick down on Harold Spencer's head and immediately, blood, lots of it, began flowing. The killer didn't stop and brought the brick down three more times. *The bastard had it coming for a long time! His stupid, big head busted open like a pumpkin.*

Go out the way you came in. No one is going to see you with the thick hedge on the other side of the driveway. Go back to the bar, have one more before closing, drive home and forget it.

I want you to look at this, Mr. Evans," Lt. Riley said, as she pulled folded sheets of paper from her purse. "These are a few pages which weren't soaked in blood."

Evans examined and slid the papers back across his desk. "Wait, there *is* something. These are fake listings. The pictures of the houses don't match the addresses."

"How can they be faked?"

"By using the copier, you copy pictures of any active listings and different listing statements, glue the pieces together and run 'em through the copier again."

"If Spencer was calling people who're under contract ... I know that's illegal, Mr. Evans."

"Harold took risks and a lot of times it paid off."

"And still you kept him."

Just then, Evans' office door opened, one of the forensic men came in, followed by an invisible cloud of chlorine bleach. "We got it as cleaned up out there the best we could. The phonebook he was using—"

"—reverse directory," Evans interrupted.

"Anyhow, you're gonna hafta get another one. It was covered in blood.

"The ME's gone and we picked up our evidence, so we'll be going now, Lieutenant."

"Be sure to call us if you find anything interesting. Call us here."

"Mr. Evans," Lupinski asked, "is there a conference room with a phone?"

Evans nodded.

"When we get a call from the lab, can you transfer it to that room?"

"I don't ... our secretary can do that."

"Which one is it? The officer can go out and get her."

"She's the redhead sitting in that Plymouth.

"Tell me, either of you, are you closer to finding out who did it? Any hunches?"

The Lt. sighed, then answered, "Hunches, intuition, guesses, are all irrelative. The evidence and *only* the evidence will tell us. Okay?

"What we have here, simply is a crime of passion and most murders are committed either for love or money or, lack thereof. Then, there's motive and opportunity.

"Now, I want to talk to the person who sits in front of Spencer. Are there any women who sit near him?"

"I have four women and none of them sit near him."

"*Only* four women? You'd better work on that."

Lupinski coughed into his fist to stifle a laugh.

"Jack Moffitt sits in front of him."

"Take the uniform, excuse me, the officer with you. We'll be waiting in the conference room."

Moffitt's anxious questions were answered by Riley and Lupinski as quickly as Moffitt asked them. He took a seat opposite the detectives and draped his raincoat over the back of the chair next to him.

"Why would someone want to kill him? I know he was a complete jerk, but …"

"That's beside the point now, isn't it? It happened and we're going to find out who did it."

"Well, *I* didn't do it!"

Lt. Riley leaned forward, looking at Moffitt's raincoat. "Looks like you've got a button missing."

"Yeah, I thought I was going to be late to the Tuesday meeting, but it didn't start on time. I was in a hurry unbuttoning my raincoat and accidentally popped the bottom one off."

"Is this it?" Riley held the button up, then slid it toward Moffitt.

"Wow! I didn't know where it went. Where did you find it?"

"Near Harold Spencer's desk."

"Thanks. I'll have my wife sew it back on."

"Of course," she said and pulled a pocket notebook from her purse and furiously began scribbling notes.

Lupinski and Moffitt whispered about the weather.

Riley rose and opened the door. "Mr. Moffitt, you can go now and your co-workers *will* ask you what we're doing here, feel free to tell them. It won't make any difference."

"You told him to go?" Lupinski asked, incredulously.

"He didn't do it." Riley said, "his demeanor told me he didn't."

T hree hours had passed, thirteen real estate agents were interviewed, sent to wait in their cars and told not to leave. Some were allowed back in to use the restrooms. Lupinski and Riley waited for the lab to call.

Lupinski: "What did you write in your notes?"

Riley laughed: "See for yourself."

"Doodles? You were drawing doodles?"

"What good would notes do? *Most* of them obviously had a motive for killing the guy. Only *one* actually did and we're going to sit here 'til the lab calls and then we'll know."

Evans opened the door. "How much longer is this gonna take? My people wanna come back in."

"As long as it takes," Riley answered, "and when it's over, you can send them home. Then, you can lock-up and do the same."

The redheaded receptionist knocked on the open door. "Excuse me, but I've got the police lab on the phone."

Riley: "Transfer it in here."

Both the receptionist and Evans went back to whatever they were doing, which was nothing, but waiting.

Riley took the call: "What? Are you sure? Positive?"

Lupinski: "What is it? What'd they say?"

Riley: "Our suspect is a woman we'd interviewed. I'm completely surprised. She was so calm."

"Are you gonna tell me, or not?"

"Of course."

Riley got up, opened the door and instructed the officer to get Evans, go out to Nicole Lee's car, handcuff her and bring her in. Tell the rest of them to leave.

Lupinski: "The Korean woman? How do you know?"

"The lab said they found a few strands of long hair near the victim. Bleach-blond ... Asian."

"Why Asian?"

Riley explained that when the hair was examined under a microscope, it was round and Asians have round hair.

"I had no idea, Steve, and I bet you didn't, either."

"How many kinds of hair are there?"

"Okay, Asians have round hair, Caucasians have oval and African Americans have flat hair. Isn't science wonderful?"

"Yeah, it makes our jobs easier. I'll ride in the uniform's car and meet you at the county jail. "Mr. Evans you can lock-up after we leave. Looks like you're not gonna do any business today."

"Wait," Evans said, sounding panicked, "Lieutenant, can you keep this out of the media? I don't want any adverse publicity."

"That's not our job. It's *yours*."

The Weatherman

ollowing another unremarkable evening's work, Jack Thompson walked around the corner to his favorite bar for his usual, self-imposed limit of two martinis. Then, he would walk the three short blocks to his apartment, snap on the TV and either catch the last, few minutes of *Carson*, or an old, late-night movie.

Sam, the bartender, who'd been there forever, it seemed, rose from his stool and hobbled over to where Jack was sitting at the end of the bar.

"Your usual, Mr. Thompson?"

"Yeah, how're your legs, today?"

"Getting worse every day," Sam sighed. "Damned arthritis!"

"Hey, Sam," Jack whispered, "is that a new face sitting at the middle of the bar?"

Sam nodded, "I think so. First time I seen her."

She had been staring at Jack, but he was busy scanning the few others who were in the bar and didn't notice, at first. When their eyes met, she quickly looked away, fingering and tossing her long, luxurious, dark hair.

"Sam," Jack whispered, again, "whatever she's drinking, I'll buy her one more."

Sam groaned as he walked over to her and exchanged a few words. "Windsor, water, rocks," he repeated.

With drink in hand, Jack moved confidently toward the empty stool beside her. "My name's Jack Thompson. What's yours?"

"Did the fact that you bought me a drink, give you license to come and sit next to me?" she said, eyes narrowing.

"No," Jack answered, laughing, "but, your acceptance *implies* license."

"You win," she said, feigning boredom, "my name's Maggie and I already know who you are."

"I bought you a drink because you're the youngest, prettiest woman in here," Jack explained.

"Younger, I am. Except for you and I, all the rest in here look like walking, talking corpses. And, as far as pretty, who else would you consider buying a drink for? The woman with the glass eye and three teeth, or that ancient one with the dowager's hump? Or, how about the lady who just passed out in that booth? Poor things!"

"But, Maggie ... "

"Okay, ceasefire," Maggie laughed. "You're kind of attractive, yourself and you have a very pleasant voice. The kinds of things they're looking for, in television, I suppose. I can't imagine they'd hire anyone who's homely with a terrible voice. By the way, I couldn't help noticing that you're still wearing your makeup."

"I'll remove it when I get home, but thanks," he said. "I guess, as they say, we're establishing rapport with each other. You know that I'm the weatherman on Channel 6. What do you do?"

"I'm a professional barfly who picks up strange men."

"That's funny. Now, what do you *really* do?"

"Listen, Jack, I don't want to play this anymore. I'm just waiting for you to do the customary thing and invite me up to your place for a nightcap."

"Yeah, okay. Just like Nick and Nora Charles getting smashed before they solved homicides."

"I like the simile," she said. "We're walking there, right? It must be nice, living and working in such close proximity."

When they arrived at Jack's apartment, Maggie made a beeline for the sofa, while he started making drinks.

"Nice place, beautiful view, the Spartan décor absolutely suits you," she observed. "Anything at all that you're having would be fine," she said, pointing toward the liquor. "So, how long have you been doing the, I mean *reporting* the weather?"

"I came to KMOG in 1960, so about four years," he said, handing her a drink.

"*Four years?*" She gave him a piercing stare with her dark eyes. "How old *are* you? You don't look like an old man! You still have a full head of hair, with no trace of gray and you have most of your teeth. My dear Jack, have you looked in the mirror, lately?"

"I'm thirty-two," he said, slightly perturbed, "and I don't know what you're talking about."

"Then tell me, how do you get your weather information? Doppler Radar? Are the maps shown on a *green screen*? You sit in the newsroom. What's the latest news in the mid-1960s?"

"I still don't know what you're talking about," he answered defensively, "some of your questions I can address, but I've never heard of, what was it? 'Doppler Radar' and 'green screen'? We get our information from the National Weather Service via teletype then, we transcribe it and apply it to the broadcast. Our maps are large, opaque pieces of plexiglass and, from behind it, one of our stagehands draws clouds, or sun, or lightning bolts, or tornadoes and writes temperatures backwards with a grease pen. And, of course, the latest news is the increasing U.S. troop strength in Southeast Asia. There have you got it, now?"

"If you fast-forward fifty years," Maggie began, "you'd be amazed at what the hot topics are, nowadays. And you can wear plaid, it doesn't bleed, and stripes won't strobe with high-definition TV. But, remember the green screen? You can never wear green. What you've been delivering all this time, is very old news … repeating the same four years over and over, ad infinitum."

"Lady, you're crazy! Just who the hell are you? I think you'd better leave, now!"

"Not without you, my dear." she said, "look around … the same few people are *always* in that bar and it's a Friday night. And you and the bartender are the only *men* in there. Where *is* everyone? Look out the window. There's only five people walking around … the traffic. Since I've been here, I've counted a grand total of three cars! And, did it ever occur to you why it's always dark outside? When was the last time you saw sunlight?"

"I'm having another drink, then I'm throwing you out. But first, if you know, or have some kind of logical explanation of what you *think* is going on, then either tell me, or stop talking!"

"It's not only what *I* believe," she explained, "it's what I know as absolute fact. It's also the reason why I'm here to tell you what's real and what isn't. Your perception of reality is real only to *you*."

"Are you saying that none of this or, my environment is real? And that some of us are standing still while the rest have been moving forward?"

"Not exactly," she said, with more sincerity, "but, you're getting warmer. Do you ever wonder that you don't have to get your haircut, anymore? That neither your fingernails, nor your beard grows, and you don't get hammered on alcohol, anymore? You never even have to go to the bathroom! You don't need sleep. Perhaps you only lay in bed and pretend. If we went back to that bar, we'd find that it doesn't exist. Oh, it used to exist … That place, the people in it, this apartment and the TV studio were created by you from your memory. All illusory images.

"Do you want to know what you've been refusing to believe all these years? It's something that happened to you in 1964. Since you deny that anything happened, I'm going to tell you. You were sent out, during a thunderstorm, to do a promo for your weather segment. There you were, wearing a lavalier microphone, a perfect lightning rod, when you were struck by a bolt of lightning. It took out your cameraman, too."

"It sounds as if you're suggesting that we're … dead!" The words, coming from Jack's lips were barely audible. He could hardly believe he was saying it.

"Not you and I, Jack," Maggie said, as she stood, "it's you. Are you ready to leave, now? You don't belong here. Please, just take my hand."

Squirrels

It was on one uneventful Saturday afternoon that I found a large, unopened bag of peanuts lying on the kitchen table. My plan was to watch a football game on TV, eat some peanuts while waiting for my wife to come home from work. I love salted-in-the-shell peanuts, but when I cracked the first one, it was raw. I ate it anyway, thinking it was anomalous and ate another. That too, was raw and at that point, gave up.

When Myrna came home, I asked what was wrong with the goddam peanuts.

"They're not for you, they're for the squirrels."

"The squirrels?"

"Yeah, Mike, I've almost got them taking peanuts from my hand."

I already felt that our yard was being overrun by these tree-dwelling rodents and she was encouraging these *nature's beggars*. "Oh, they're so cute," she'd say. I didn't agree.

When we first met, I agreed with everything she did and said. Love makes you do crazy, irrational things … like marrying Myrna.

Her love affair with the squirrels continued until she heard some rustling sounds coming from the attic. She investigated and found a dozen pairs of beady-eyed demons staring at her.

"I'm calling animal rescue," she announced, "it's the humane thing to do."

"Humane? What the hell are you talking about? Why don't you just attach your car's tailpipe to the attic vent? Then, when they're all dead, scoop 'em up into a garbage bag with a snow shovel."

"That's right. Spoken like a true squirrel-hater. Have you lost your sense of decency? I don't want to *hurt* my little friends."

The guy from animal rescue went into the attic and sprayed some mild, sensory irritant, or something, and said that it was, "all fixed." All it did was chase them out of the attic and back into the yard.

My wife began spending too much time playing in the yard with her friends. When Myrna starting climbing trees, it made me believe that she'd regressed into childhood. Certainly, after ten years of marriage, I've never witnessed behavior so bizarre.

27

One day, I was shocked to see that she'd given herself a buzz cut. It made her ears appear higher than usual. And was it my imagination, or were her eyes moving closer to the sides of her head? When she ate, she rotated food with her, slender, long-nailed fingers and took small nibbles. Her two front teeth seemed to be getting longer.

I didn't get a chance to ask her what was going on. Besides, I didn't want to *assume* anything. And then, she inexplicably left home.

It had been nearly a year since she left, without telling me why and without telling me if she was ever coming back. There wasn't anything I could do about it ... except worry about her all the time.

One night, I clicked off the TV and picked up a book. It didn't matter if I read it twice before. After turning off all the lights except for a small reading lamp next to my lounge chair, I settled back. The sound of scratching on the front door had wakened me. It was midnight. I hadn't even finished the first chapter.

I went to the door and flung it open, hoping to see what was making that noise. It was a squirrel about the size of a chihuahua. Before I could slam the door, it ran across the room, hopped onto the sofa and sat on its haunches, staring at me.

"Myrna, is that you?"

The *Myrna-squirrel* chirped, in what sounded to me like an affirmation. There was more scratching at the door, I opened it and her brood of six young squirrels rushed in.

Every evening at midnight, for several years hence, all of them came to visit me and together, we sat on the couch and ate raw peanuts.

The Novel

Hunched over the keyboard, I paused for a moment. Thinking of the best words to use, was perhaps, my most daunting task.

My wife came into the room, stood next to the monitor and faced me, arms akimbo.

"Jerry, are you going to do that all summer? You know the trim on the house needs painting and here you sit."

"I'm working on this science-fiction novel … "

"What do you know about science? You teach seventh-grade Humanities to a bunch of mouth-breathing, slack-jawed imbeciles."

"They're not *that* bad."

"Oh, no? You told me that one kid's essay explained that, during the Civil War, when the Confederacy ran out of money, it delayed their missile program. So, there you go."

"Well, I have to admit that some of them are like that."

"May I see what you've written, so far? *Mars?* Why is it that it's always aliens from Mars landing on Earth? That's so *hack!* Why does it have to be science-fiction? Why can't it be a normal story taking place in, say, South Dakota? Take a break, your lunch is ready and why are you smoking? You *know* it's bad for the computer!"

"Okay, I'll be there in a minute."

She left the room with a sigh. Maybe Susan had a point. Maybe it *should* take place in South Dakota. I could have archaeologists, a thousand years into the future, examining Mount Rushmore and wonder if aliens carved the presidents' heads and have them liken that structure with the pyramids and Stonehenge.

Or, *wow!* I could have aliens, from a distant galaxy, landing near Rushmore, thousands of years into the future. That's it!

I decided that the best time to write would be when she's at work, or when she's sleeping, *not* on weekends.

What began only as a hobby, my writing had grown into an obsession, motivated by wanting to move into a larger house and being able to afford it. And, what we've talked about the last couple of years; having a child or two.

The following Monday, I cracked my knuckles and resumed writing my novel.

At the dinner table, that evening, I gave a brief explanation of what I had written. She feigned interest and replied, "Still sticking to the science-fiction genre?"

"Yes, it worked for L. Ron Hubbard."

"He wasn't best known for his writing," she huffed, "he was known for inventing a new *religion*."

"Well, maybe *I'll* invent a new religion, too!"

"What, aliens as ancient gods? That's already been done."

I continued writing every weekday. The weekends were reserved for the various chores that Susan had chosen for me to accomplish. By mid-August, I had written and rewritten about three-hundred pages. School was going to start in about three week and I had to bang out four-hundred more pages, otherwise it would be a novella and that wouldn't do. It would mean that I'd have to work on it, through the weekends and late every night.

The aliens had discovered a *wormhole*, through which they traveled at many times the speed of light, allowing them to arrive on Earth in only a few years, instead of centuries. When they left their planet, they believed that Earth was still inhabited, but when they landed, they found a desolate planet; overgrown jungles in some areas and large deserts in other parts.

The aliens looked up, from the foot of Mount Rushmore. They could see that the carved faces had been eroded by time and the elements into vague representations, their features nearly obliterated. They wondered what it was and why it was there. Did the former inhabitants build this object to honor four of their most powerful gods? Only their heads? Why not the entire bodies? Did the people *look* like their gods?

The aliens began looking for artifacts, or anything which may contain clues to this planet's long-passed civilization.

After a few hours, they unearthed skeletal remains of what they thought was that of a typical inhabitant. It was quite large, had four legs and an elongated skull. The aliens found several others of the same and concluded that this was the primary race of beings. They took note of how different those beings appeared, in comparison to their gods.

A short distance away, they found the remnants of another god—some sort of stone monument. This one appeared to be sitting upon the back of a creature they had identified as a member of the *primary race*. They found this very curious, indeed.

In another area, they saw, sticking out of the sand, a long, wooden object. One of them pulled it out, examined the symbols on which were engraved, "Louisville Slugger" and telepathically transmitted the information to the ship's computer for deciphering. What sort of beings were they and what use and purpose was this piece of wood?

Susan came into the room and asked, "Are you done for today?"

"I'm almost done with the whole thing."

"Did you remember to send a query letter to the publisher?"

"Yes, I sent one a week ago."

At the end of November, I received a reply from the publisher. It was a handwritten note explaining that my novel wasn't the genre in which they were interested in publishing, but that perhaps a memoir would be more appealing to readers.

I discarded the note and began rewriting my novel as a personal memoir.

The main character was myself, as one of the aliens and Susan was the commander of the spaceship, barking orders.

"Hurry up, down there! We can't stay here forever! Besides, there's no civilization left and the atmosphere is corrosive!"

The Revolt

I t had been three decades since the war ended. The losing side called it a "war," the winners, the government, called it a "revolt," which they had *extinguished* in less than a week.

"Michael," Michael's grandfather called, "can you stop what you're doing and come here? I want to talk to you?"

"Sure, Grandpa, what is it?"

"Remember when you were just a little boy, I started taking you into the woods where we target practiced with different kinds of guns?"

"Yeah," Michael said, grinning. "I thought it was only a game," his grin disappeared, "but, then I found out what its purpose was. Why do you ask?"

"Because, you're old enough now, eighteen, right? And your mission, the one for which you've trained for so long, is about to come to fruition. Tomorrow night, when you go to work in the city, you're to stay after curfew, imposed on *outsiders*, and loiter in Sector 8."

"But, I'm not allowed to stay after curfew, especially in *that* sector, since I don't work there."

"That, Michael, is the idea. That's where you'll meet your contact. The police will arrest you and you'll spend the rest of the night in jail."

"Will I meet my contact, then?"

"Yes, he'll be a detective, Captain McCarthy. He's about forty, heavyset, shaved head and he has a scar running from the bridge of his nose, across his right cheek. You're to talk to no one else. Do you understand?"

"Yes, I do."

"And you understand that your mission is to be involved in the assassination of the Midwest Regional Governor. I'm not aware of the *extent* of your involvement, or how dangerous it'll be, but you'll be briefed further by McCarthy. There are a handful of other cops who're also on our side."

"Grandpa, I'm ready for this. I think I've *always* been ready. It's all about resisting the enemy. That's what you've taught me and you told me that my parents sacrificed themselves exactly for that reason."

The old man shook his head and sighed, "Yes, my daughter, my son-in-law *and* your grandmother knew what they were getting into. I was lucky, but they paid the price ... "

The city dwellers were government loyalists, while the rebels were called "outsiders," a term of derision, when spoken by city dwellers.

Michael had also known, for a long time, that his paternal grandparents were city dwellers; the enemy.

Moments after midnight, Michael was found, sitting on a curb, by two large, muscular, uniformed cops, a man and a woman. The woman asked him for his papers. "This is a *work* permit!" she yelled toward the other cop, even though he was standing directly in front of her. "You're an *outsider*! I could tell right away by your shabby clothes and that disgusting *long hair*! And besides being out after curfew, you're in the wrong sector! You're only permitted to work in Sector 5! Let's go, get in the car! Pat him down and cuff him," she told the male cop.

Michael didn't resist or say a word. At the police station, he was turned over to the jailer who took him to a dingy, two-man cell which was already occupied by an old man.

"Your arraignment is next week," the jailer laughed, "lotsa luck."

The old man rose from his cot. "So, what are you in for, kid?"

"Being out after curfew."

"Oh, yeah? Same here. My name's Al, what's yours?"

Michael hesitated, then said, "Jack. My name's Jack."

This guy could be a plant. *The cell is probably bugged. He's got long hair and* looks *like an outsider* ...

"Sorry, man. I've had a rough night and I don't feel like talking. I just wanna get some sleep."

He lay down on the other cot, across from the man and wondered that if something went wrong, or they had to abort the plan, what would happen to *him*? How dangerous would it be?

The next morning, a thin man, not much older than Michael, appeared outside the cell with a jailer. "Let that one out," pointing at Michael.

The thin man was a cop, a detective. This one wasn't wearing a suitcoat so that his gun, a 9 mm and his badge were plainly visible on his belt.

"Come with me. The Captain wants to see you."

"Captain McCarthy?" Michael asked.

The cop didn't answer and motioned Michael to walk with him. They went upstairs and entered a small, austere office. A large man, whom Michael's grandfather accurately described as, "McCarthy," was sitting behind a desk. McCarthy stood and said, "We're gonna take a little ride in my car." Michael felt the cold steel on his wrists as handcuffs were applied.

The thin cop drove, Michael was placed in the backseat and McCarthy sat in the front. They arrived at a city park, stopped, with the car idling. No one spoke for a few minutes when suddenly, the thin cop turned and pointed his 9 mm at Michael's forehead.

"What're you *doing*?" Michael shouted.

"Sorry, kid," McCarthy said, "but, this is what we do with outsider, rebel scum."

"Don't you know what I'm here to do? I'm *one* of you!"

"Sure you are," the thin cop said, as he tightened his grip on the gun.

Somebody lied *to me! Who* lied? *No it* couldn't *have been* Grandpa! *Why would he* betray *me?*

"I've been setup. So, pull the trigger, asshole! I'm not afraid!"

Inexplicably, the cop with the gun, smiled. McCarthy glanced at his partner and said, "Put it away and take the cuffs off." At Michael he asked, "Did you notice that the safety was on? Probably not. Do you want some water?"

Michael uttered a barely audible, "Yeah," and was handed a water bottle.

"Well," McCarthy said in a relaxed tone, "that was the *second* test you passed."

"The second?" Michael asked between gulps of water. "What was the first?"

"Your cellmate. I put him there. He's been with us for years. You didn't say too much to him and that's exactly what we expected from you."

"He works for you?"

"We work together."

"So, how come the police are involved in all this?"

"Because, we're not likely to arouse suspicion and we have more access to different places. Now, let's get down to business. Have you ever fired a .45?"

"Yes."

"Good. We're going back to the station and discuss the plan."

McCarthy showed Michael a different cell in the sub-basement, one with an iron door. "I hope you don't mind these accommodations," McCarthy said, "you won't be watched down here. It'll only be 'til tomorrow afternoon. You'll find everything you need in those two paper bags; a black pair of pants, a black, light wool sweater and, in the other bag, a hair-trimmer and a .45. You'll be giving yourself a buzz cut to blend in with the crowd. The sweater is big enough to conceal the .45 in your waistband."

McCarthy and Michael sat on a cot and McCarthy continued, "I know that your grandfather had told you a little bit about your mission, but not everything. First of all, *you'll* be the primary shooter. Tomorrow's Sunday and the Governor will be in the city to give a speech or, some kind of sermon. When he's done and steps away from the podium, you'll run toward him and fire the .45 as many times as it takes to bring him down. You won't have time to aim, so just point the weapon at his chest. Believe me, it's gonna leave some very big holes!"

"But, if there's a large crowd, how can I get close enough?"

"Remember the woman cop who arrested you? She's the one who'll lead you to the right position, then she'll step a few feet away and stay there 'til you begin moving forward."

"So, I shoot the Governor, then what happens?"

"Our policewoman will rush toward you and shoot you twice."

"What? What the hell are you saying?"

"Relax. Her first two rounds are blanks. They'll have a heavier powder charge so it'll sound like the real thing. She's gonna point her weapon at your stomach, fire twice and you'll fall to the ground. The rest of the cops will surround your supposedly dead body 'til an ambulance arrives and takes you away. Your action is a signal for the other regions to begin assassinations of *their* Governors."

"So, then the revolt will finally begin?"

"Yes and you'll be remembered as a patriot ... a hero, except that you'll also be remembered as a martyr."

"How're people supposed to believe I'm dead?"

"No one will see any blood because of your black sweater. The EMT's who're working with us, will scoop you up and drive you to an airfield where you'll board a flight, out of the country. I'm not at liberty to tell you, right now, exactly where you're going. It's part of our *protection program* and you'll be given a new identity."

"Will I ever see my grandpa, again? Will I ever be able to come home?"

"You can't see your grandpa anytime soon, but we'll see if we can arrange a trip for him in about a year. And you *must* realize, Michael, that the whole world will assume that you're dead, so, no, you'll never be able to return. Since you've been in deep cover all this time, we'll be issuing a statement to the media. It'll say that your remains were cremated and your ashes scattered.

"And we'll create a fake bio, stating that you acted alone; that you were a crazy misfit. We'll even interview some former schoolteachers and have them say that you were a poor student and an angry loner. Your grandpa will say something similar and your city-dweller grandparents, if we pay them, will say that you were a misguided youth and blame your outsider grandfather. City dwellers will lie about anything if you pay them. Well, I think I've answered most of your questions and concerns. I'll see you tomorrow. Good luck to you."

"Yeah, I'll need it!"

The following day, Michael heard a rasping, metallic sound and knew someone was unlocking his cell door. It was the jailer who let him out the first time. "Are you ready?" he asked. Michael nodded. "Don't worry," the jailer added, "your hair will grow back before you know it."

Small consolation ... if I have a head left, on which to grow it!

A last-minute check to see if the clip was full, Michael slid a round into the chamber.

As he left the police station, he could hear the throng of people already gathering. There, he met the policewoman and walked silently behind her. With her hand, she made a slight, nearly imperceptible, motion to where he was supposed to stand.

The Governor took his place at the podium and raised his hands to silence the cheering crowd. He then, launched into his speech.

Michael noticed some uniformed police standing behind the Governor and a few detectives, in rumpled suits, standing there, as well, included McCarthy and his partner.

The speech droned on for about twenty minutes and when it was over, the Governor turned to his left and began walking away from the podium.

Now! Michael said to himself and reached under his sweater. He started to run forward, when he heard the loud crack of a rifle. It was difficult to determine the direction of the shot, in the canyon of buildings, but he thought it came from a rooftop. A micro-second later, the Governor began to slump. *A head shot*, Michael realized as he kept running forward, taking out the .45. He pointed and fired off three shots into the Governor, yelling loudly, "This is for you, you crazy bastard!"

Everything, from that point on, moved with purpose and precision. The policewoman fired her two shots at Michael and helped the other cops keep bystanders away.

McCarthy ran to the ambulance and got into the back as Michael was pushed in on a gurney. "Does it hurt much?" McCarthy asked, "I bet it *does*."

"You dirty motherfuckers!" cried Michael, "those weren't *blanks!*"

"Of course not. You were right. You *were* setup. Not by your grandpa. Oh, well, I might as well tell you that he died about a half-hour ago."

"You had him *killed?*"

"Yeah, we had to."

"What about the other shooter?"

"He never made it off the rooftop. We got him. He was part of the plot, as well. Governors can always be replaced, but if we don't stop the assassins, eventually they might stop *us*."

McCarthy ordered the ambulance to pull over and stop. "Take this kid out," he growled, "and put him on the ground." He drew his gun and fired one, fatal shot into Michael's head, jammed the gun back into his holster and muttered to himself, "Now, we can keep this great country the way it was intended."

Freedom Rider

I f it wasn't for Country singer Merle Haggard's 1969 hit, "Okie from Muskogee," most of us would never have heard of the place.

During World War Two, the nearest town to Camp Gruber was Muskogee, Oklahoma. My dad, a Staff Sergeant in the Army, was stationed there a short time and was in charge of the motor pool. He was accompanied to Oklahoma by my mom and my brother, Dennie, who was a year old at the time.

Even with Muskogee's housing shortage, they had found a duplex and rented the upstairs.

The story, or incident, of what happened in Muskogee on a steamy, summer day in 1943, was told to me many times by my mom and corroborated by my dad, albeit from a different perspective.

She, along with my brother, had boarded a city bus, crowded with townsfolk and soldiers. There was one seat left toward the front. She took it and held my brother on her lap. A little farther along, the bus stopped to pick up a young, pregnant African American woman, or "colored gal," as they said back then.

The woman had no place to sit until my mom stood and offered to give up her seat. The woman gratefully accepted, to the audible gasps of the rest of the passengers. The driver paused for a long time, looked back and gave my mom a baleful glare, along with the other white people on board.

Of course my white, Yankee mom was deliberately disregarding the "Jim Crow" laws which relegated blacks, in all cases, to the back of the bus. She got away with what many Southerners would consider a crime; not just a social faux pas.

At the time, Jim Crow was the law of the land, supported by the "Separate but Equal" doctrine which had been cheerfully upheld by the U.S. Supreme Court in countless appeals. This was racial segregation, Southern style.

When my mom told my dad what had happened, he blew his cork.

"Ruth, don't you understand? I'm in the Army!"

"So are a lot of other men. What are you saying?"

"I'm sayin' … and don't you tell our busybody landlady or anybody else … I'm sayin' I'll probably get hauled in front of the Provost Marshal and tossed in the stockade. I'll be wearin' a 'P' on my back for the rest of the war!"

"You're exaggerating, Don. Besides, I did what Mrs. Roosevelt would've done; which is the right thing."

"You're not Mrs. Roosevelt! Look, you know and I know you did the right thing, but things are different down here. You just better lay low 'til this thing blows over, or we're gonna have more trouble than we can handle."

About a decade later, Rosa Parks stepped onto a bus in Montgomery, Alabama.

Last Will

Dear Gerald,

I'll be eighty-nine this year, before it's too late and still have my wits about me, I'm planning on visiting my attorney and drawing up a will.

You, being my ne'er-do-well nephew and last surviving relative, must read this letter and carefully process what I'm telling you.

Even though I've become a successful businessman, you and your family never had anything to do with me. I doubt if either of your parents ever told you this, but I've posted your bail three times. I offered to put you through college, too. Evidently, your parents didn't tell you that either, because you dropped out of high school and hitchhiked to California. When you didn't want to hitchhike back home, you asked your parents for airfare. You knew they couldn't afford it and were upset when they sent you a bus ticket.

After getting a job at a service station rimming tires, you married a divorced, older woman with two kids. When she divorced you, your child support payments fell into arrears and I anonymously paid them at least ten times.

It became overwhelmingly obvious that she was a gold digger and when she figured out you had no gold, she dumped you.

I wish I was in a position to offer you some solid investment advice, but whenever I tried to connect with you, you drifted farther away. Then again, perhaps it's not your fault ... or mine. Maybe it's your parents' fault. Over the years, I've tried to reach out to help them financially, but they just blew me off. Worse yet, they *ignored* me! I'll never understand why some people are so prideful as to refuse any level of charity when it's offered.

Your dad, while suffering from mid-life crisis, ran away from home and your mom, my dear, younger sister, died as you were growing into adulthood. So, you had no one to be your mentor, your counselor.

I don't think you're stupid, but I *do* worry about your mental stability.

I'll put my hand out to you just one more time. Over my lifetime, I've made a lot of money and spent a lot of money. Having a Will means, that upon my death, I won't have to give any of it to the government.

After I settle certain expenses and burial costs, I'll have approximately ten million dollars to give you. If you spend it wisely, it should last a lifetime.

Wait a minute … I've read and seen several murder mysteries where a character can't wait for an old geezer to croak and murders him to get the whole amount right away. After all, who wants to wait an indeterminable amount of time to get rich?

Here's my offer: I'll give you one million now and that should last you until I die. The nine million will be given to you at the time of my demise. How does that sound?

On the other hand, I've thought it over. I'll be giving the entire ten million to a few of my favorite charities and you, Gerald, can go fuck yourself.

Inauguration

"**W**hat happened to all those people?" my ten-year-old daughter asked.

After a few moments I said, "I don't know." She stared at me, wanting more than that. I had nothing more. Millions of people around the world saw what happened and no one who believed their own eyes, could believe what they'd witnessed.

The Chief Justice of the Supreme Court stood at the lectern, ready to administer the oath of office; the new president, at the lectern's opposite. Next to the president, the First Lady was holding a Bible.

"Raise your right hand and repeat after me," the judge bellowed.

The president pushed his way past his wife, knocking her back into her chair, and began speaking to the crowd. The judge returned to his seat.

"Look at this. Will you look at this? I tell ya folks, this is so unnecessary. All this hoopla! For what? Let's just get this over with, huh?

"You want me to give a speech, right?" A wave of cheers rose from the crowd. "This will be the greatest speech you'll ever hear. In fact, the greatest speech you'll ever *need* to hear." More cheers.

"I stand before you, the humblest of servants, ready for whatever awaits us in the future after so much divisiveness in this country. I don't intend to mete-out punishment for all the non-believers, but I know what's in their hearts and I know what's in *your* hearts, my loyal followers. And so, I make this promise: I can and shall take you to the promised land and you're deserving of it. All those who're with me, raise your hands." Most waved and cheered, while some looked at each other quizzically.

"Folks, I have to tell you that I'm known by many, many names. Some, I can hardly pronounce. And I've walked among you before, but this time, I'm going to change how it ends. I'm going to *reward* those who were the most loyal. I have immense power. That I can tell you and I'll show you with this little demonstration."

Gesturing with his left hand ... the hand he would've placed on the Bible. The obelisk, otherwise known as the Washington Monument, began to shake and groan. It started to tear away from its mortise anchors and tenon joints. Then it levitated for a moment, before making its ascent into the darkling sky. Picking up velocity, it disappeared out of sight.

"What're you looking at, people? It's not going to come back down. Not *ever* coming down.

"There's something I want to say to those who voted for me; I love all of you, but I've got to say that I knew I could depend on your gullibility. And to those who *didn't* vote for me; you don't know what you'll be missing. And to *all* of you; you ain't seen *nothin'*, yet!"

He looked behind him at the gallery, then on his left at three former presidents and their wives. "This is something that *you* will never see again, either. I can tell you that."

Then, he looked to his right at the vice president. "And you're coming along, aren't you?" The vice president nodded.

"It's been a long, bumpy ride, but soon, very soon it'll be over. I promise you it'll be painless. Think of it as the *rapture* in reverse."

A black, dense cloud inched its way down The Mall, toward the capitol and hovered over the mass of people.

The president's fists shot upward, his hair looked like it was on fire. The cloud descended, first to the gallery, then to ground level. The president took his vice president's arm and said, "You're going to meet a lot of interesting historical people. Don't look so bewildered."

The dark cloud grew lighter, dissipated and thousands of people disappeared. There were screams, crying and whimpering from the people who were spared. Then, a swelling of relief, followed by deafening cheers.

"**B**ut, where *did* they go, Dad?"

"Well, that's just something about which to speculate. One thing for sure though, is that it's a new day and I've got a feeling that everything's going to be okay, now."

Intervention

herapy shopping, I'd always called it. I found it especially appropriate on my thirtieth birthday. I didn't enjoy the prospect of being a middle-aged mall rat, but I had to either celebrate the first thirty years of life, or bitch about the inevitability of not yet becoming a millionaire.

It began as a normal, summer Saturday. Bill was home with the girls and I, armed with a couple of hardly used platinum cards, stepped out of the car, at the mall and the nearly full parking lot. *Bill would just buy something sensible for my birthday, but I might as well indulge myself with something frivolous, like another pair of shoes.*

Suddenly, a man's voice, behind me, barely above a whisper; "Listen carefully. Don't turn around. Push the button, unlock the passenger side and get back in the driver's seat. Don't do anything else. I have a gun." I unlocked the door and froze. I finally saw him when he got into the car. He spoke again, this time louder and more commanding; "I told you to get in the car and start it."

Still startled, I stared at him for a moment. I couldn't help noticing how youthful he looked. His face was virtually creaseless, but pale, as if he hadn't been out in the sun for months. That, plus the curly, copper-red hair, made him look even younger. So, I said something *very* foolish: "If you've got a gun, show it to me."

He pulled a shiny, small caliber, semi-automatic pistol out of his black suitcoat and showed it to me, holding it beneath the dashboard.

I feigned shock, touched my fingers to my lips and gasped. At that point, I didn't want to get angry in public because it would be both messy and horrifying. He smiled a little and said, "Buckle up. Let's get going."

My curiosity was piqued and I wanted to see where this situation was headed.

"Who are you and what do you want? Money?" I reached for my purse, but he grabbed it and placed it on the floor, between his feet.

"Trying to get your cell phone? You won't need anything in your purse. Now, take a left onto the highway. I'll direct you from there."

Left on the highway, then where?

"Maintain the speed limit. Not over, not under." He patted the pocket with the gun for added emphasis. I nodded my head, but didn't speak. I was pretty certain that my mounting anger would reveal itself in my voice and I didn't want him to hear that.

"Where are we going?"

"You'll see when we get there."

We're still heading West. As soon as I thought it, he told me to turn right at the next light, then another left. *We were going West again to who knows where for who knows what.*

I drove for about seventy miles when he broke the silence and said, motioning with his arm, "Turn left on that dirt road and slow down. And why are you looking in the rearview mirror? Nobody's following us."

I covered my eyes and pretended to cry.

The man grimaced, his jaw tightened. "It's not what you think. See that old farmhouse? Turn in the driveway."

The house was a square, nondescript, little bungalow. Dingy, white curtains, in the picture window; the only window in the front of the house, were pulled closed. When we both were out of the car, I saw that he was, maybe, a couple of inches shorter than I. As he unlocked the door, his hands were trembling.

He motioned for me to walk in front of him. I glanced back and gave him a pleading look. "Just keep walking down this hallway," he said. His demeanor, it seemed, belied his cherubic face.

At the end of the hallway, was a windowless room with a heavy-looking, steel plated door which stood ajar. He pushed me into the room and locked the door, followed by a scraping sound, like metal on metal. Of course, he slid a bar across, for good measure.

"What if I have to go to the bathroom? This house has a bathroom. I saw it."

"No running water and no electricity. There's a plastic pail in the corner," he yelled back. "I'll return later. And no use screaming, no one's going to hear you."

Screaming was something I'd never do in any circumstance. I sat on the floor, with my back against the wall, drew my knees up, rested my head on my arms and waited. I thought of the irony of my not wanting to wear a wristwatch. So, the only way of marking time, was looking at the faint sliver of light shining through at the bottom of the door.

As the only light disappeared, enveloping me in total blackness, my thoughts were the only color in the room, as they were vivid and quite bloody.

I should take a shit in that bucket and if and when he comes back, I'll throw it in his face! I allowed myself the visual and smiled.

I found myself curled up on the floor. I'd fallen asleep. For how long? I didn't know. The room remained a black void. I felt chilled and clammy and had to piss. So, I crawled over to where I thought that bucket might've been. *Oh, the hell with it.* I pulled my jeans down, squatted and pissed on the floor. Then, I crawled back to the approximate place where I'd been sleeping and waited for that sliver of light to reappear.

Time passed and all I could think of was that punk who imprisoned me. He probably went home to his family and was living, by all appearances, a normal life.

The light under the door finally reappeared. I could see the room slightly better; the dirty white walls and the floor, painted red cement. The paint was chipped away, in places, revealing several layers of different colors. Red, apparently was the last color choice.

"I'm back." The voice at the door, was one which I recognized as that of the redheaded son of a bitch.

I walked to the door,"Yeah, and I'm still here."

"Go to the other side of the room. I'm opening the door. I brought you a couple of burgers, fries and a bottle of water."

I was hungrier than I thought and began tearing into the food. "Will you stay awhile and keep me company?" I mumbled with my mouth full.

"Well, I suppose."

"Okay. I'd really like to know a few things. Is this some kind of a hobby with you? I mean locking people up? What thrill are you getting from this? I'll bet you've done this lots of times. Oh, and by the way, where's your video camera? I could put on quite a show for you. Then, you could keep and cherish your memory of me. You could even compare me with your past and future conquests."

Looking sincerely like his feelings were hurt, "It's not ... *I'm* not like that."

"What *are* you like, then? Why don't we find out and do the beast with two backs. You know, the old in and out. Whaddaya say, sport?"

"No! Beguiler! I shall not be seduced!"

"Is it me? Or, do you hate *all* women? You know, I'm not all *that* unattractive. Yeah, my hair's a mess, makeup's worn off … I've got it. There's something wrong with you. Either that, or you're gay. Are you?"

"No! I'm leaving now. I'll be back in a couple of hours."

As he closed the door, I threw the water bottle at it. "Fuck you! No need to hurry back!" It felt good to curse, again. It had been such a longtime and also, it was a wonderful release. I knew that I had time to sharpen my repertoire, before he returned.

After the food, water and all the yelling, I had to take a shit. I looked at the pail and smiled. I had a better idea. I backed up to the bottom of the door and made a sizable deposit on the floor. When he opens the door, he'll get a nice surprise. I sat down and waited.

It could've been less than two hours, or much more, when I heard a key in the lock and the bar slide to the side. I remained seated on the floor and focused on the shit pile by the door.

The kidnapper opened the door and with his hand covering his mouth, screamed, "Oh, God! What a pig! You're a disgusting pig!"

I rolled on the floor and laughed. I stopped laughing when I saw his black shirt and white clerical collar. "You're a priest," I said, genuinely surprised, "a goddam *priest!*"

"Yes, and we're here to help you."

At the moment I thought "we," a shorter, heavyset, older man stepped into the doorway. He was balding with wispy, white hair and his demeanor was extremely somber. Like his younger counterpart, he wore a black suit, but wore a red shirt, which was also topped with the white collar of a cleric.

"Sandra," the young priest said, using my name for the first time, "this is Monsignor Kowalski. He's an expert in his field."

"What field?" I asked and stood defiantly, with my arms akimbo. "And what are you assholes up to?"

The Monsignor spoke softly, "We are here because there is evidence that you have either engaged in witchcraft, or you are demonically possessed."

"What evidence, you bilious shitsack?" I shrieked so loudly that both men covered their ears. "Wait, don't tell me, you're exorcists, right? You still believe in that bullshit?"

"To answer your first question," the young priest replied, "we prefer to call ourselves, 'interventionists,'"

"It's the same fucking thing! Who asked you to intervene and why?"

"Watch your step, Monsignor," the young priest cautioned, as they walked into the room. They still kept their distance.

The Monsignor looked directly at me and said, sternly, "First, the evidence. These are all witnessed incidents which have occurred within the last month. The last time you had attended Mass, you partook in Holy Communion. You gagged when the host was placed in your mouth and you spit it out into a tissue."

"Yes, I remember. I choked on the wafer."

The young priest said, stepping forward, "You mean the Body of Christ."

"Ah," I said, nodding, "metamorphic oral incorporation. It was a goddam *wafer*!"

Startled, the young priest stepped back.

"What else have you got?"

The Monsignor, who made it quite apparent that he was in charge, said, "You were seen conversing with a black cat."

"Ooo, a black *cat*," I chided, "so what? I also talk to birds and house plants."

"But, this was more like a conversation. You were asking it questions," the Monsignor went on, "then you would answer with a 'yes' or 'no.'"

"Okay, fine. Next." I toned it down a bit because I actually *did* want to hear more.

"You may refute this, too. You started a fire in your fireplace only by looking at it."

"There were hot embers already in there when I threw in a wadded-up newspaper," I said, through clenched teeth, anger mounting. "Hold it," I growled, "my husband didn't see me throw the newspaper in, he just saw me look back. In fact, he saw me do *all* of those things. It was *he* who asked for this so-called intervention, wasn't it?"

"Your husband asked your parish priest to recommend someone," the Monsignor explained.

My husband will get his own piece of hell when I go home! "So, he recommended you two fucking clowns!" I stepped toward them.

"Stay back," the Monsignor warned, "this is Holy Water."

He held a vial above his head and began the incantation, "In the name of the Father and of ..."

I felt a spray of water and started forward, saying as menacingly as I could, without laughing, "You boys are in way over your heads." Clearly, this sent the priests backing up in sheer panic.

"The Holy Water didn't work! Oh, no! She's starting to change, getting larger, hands turning into claws. That face, those teeth! I can't bear to look! You've got the gun, Paul," he told the priest, "use it on this beast, this succubus, and shoot to kill!" The Monsignor stumbled back and searched for his cell phone.

Paul fired three shots at me, in rapid succession, with no effect. I moved very fast, as they tried to run away. I grabbed the old one by the neck, reached out, took the young one by his hair, smashed their heads together and dragged them back into the room. As a final touch, I drove their skulls into the cement floor, again and again until I was sure that their heads were thoroughly crushed.

The floor turned out to be the right color for all the blood that was spilled. It's too bad no one thought of putting in a drain.

I tried to let my anger subside, so I could turn from the monster back to my human self, but it was difficult, considering what I wanted to do to my husband.

I thought about my young daughters, Melissa and Stephanie, and that seemed to have a calming effect. I watched some of my fur disappear, my claws retract, my jaws return to normal. So, I didn't have to wait for the cover of darkness, to lope across open fields to get home. In my monster mode, I wouldn't have been in any condition to drive a car.

Late afternoon, I'd completely changed back to normal. My clothes were shredded, so I "borrowed" some of the priests' clothes and found my car keys in one of their pockets. Fighting back the lingering anger, I started driving back home.

I found my daughters sitting on the floor playing with, what looked like parts of Bill. There was lots of blood and entrails scattered around the living room. And they were completely covered in Bill's blood.

"Do you like what we did to Dad? We were angry at what he was doing to you, so we skinned him and took his bones out."

I laughed and said, "Good job, you two! Now, you can help me bury him in the garden and we'll plant some flowers."

The Mission

Two years ago, we sought and found what appeared to be, a hospitable planet with an atmosphere comparable to our own and, coincidentally, it was also a water planet with a few sizeable continents. Not surprisingly, we discovered that it supported sentient beings.

As commander of this expeditionary ship, I gathered the six crewmen together before we entered the planet's orbit. They were hand-picked, not only for their expertise in their selected fields, but for their superior intelligence.

"Gentlemen, please take your seats. You only know part of this assignment, but not all. Our scientists tell us that the race of beings, of which we are about to come in contact, are very primitive. That's not to say they're lacking in intelligence. And they use cunning to outwit their prey.

"So, are they nothing more than violent savages?" a crewmember asked.

"From what I'm told, yes."

"Yes, but we're here to change that. If this race continues the way it's going, it'll stagnate, will not evolve, they'll weaken and become extinct. Their society consists of several close-knit tribes, so there's also the dangerous habit of in-breeding. Considering this and the fact they have a propensity for war with other tribes will no doubt accelerate their extinction.

"We have harvested your sperm cells so we can artificially inseminate the females of this race. Hopefully, with your DNA, they will evolve physically and intellectually."

"Ma'am?"

"You *will* address me as, Commander."

"Yes, Commander. How are just the five of us men supposed to inseminate the entire planet?"

"Good question. We'll go to each continent and look for the largest concentration of female beings and impregnate them. This must be done to ensure their survival. We may return in two or three generations to check on their progress. Then, we can decide if we can colonize this world."

We made three orbits before landing. Checking the atmospheric conditions, I found the mix of gases was nearly identical to our own planet. The only exception was only a one-percent increase in nitrogen. We could breathe this air. Gravitational pull was also similar. The surface temperature was ninety-three degrees and very humid.

The crewmen had several questions: "Will they think we're gods?"

"Probably not. Like the beginning of our own civilization, it's likely they'll be ruled by superstition and frightened by anything out of the ordinary. So, we have to be careful with our presentation … we don't know how they'll react, since they've never seen anybody like us, before. So, we'll walk out, wearing our flight suits and improvise. Let's take our weapons. If they pose any threat to us, we'll kill them. Understood?"

Our ship was met by a large contingent of natives. They didn't drop to their knees in supplication. They all were short, but powerfully built. They had large heads supported by thick necks. They wore, what I assumed were animal skins, as loincloths. The amount of their body hair was disturbing.

As I mentally catalogued which young, ovulating females we would impregnate, an older female pushed the others aside and stood, staring at us. A guttural murmur, seemingly of approval, came from the crowd. The female stood in front of me, first. Her stench was almost unbearable. She touched and squeezed my breasts, then grabbed my crotch. I didn't move. With her hands, she measured my hips and held her hands out to the crowd. They all laughed, because their females had wider hips. *Had I assumed correctly that she was their leader? Was this a matriarchal tribe?*

Before leaving my side, she bobbed her head, making a sniffing sound. Apparently, she never smelled anything clean, before. She reacted by sneezing. My head snapped back when she yanked my long, blond ponytail. She walked up to my First Officer, patted his chest, then grabbed *his* crotch and laughed. Of course, the whole crowd laughed.

It seemed she was finished with her "inspection," when she stepped aside and raised her hand. Suddenly, a stone-tipped spear thudded into a crewman's chest.

"Weapons! Torch this female and the one who threw the spear! Doctor, let's get this man back to the ship!"

We ran, carrying the fallen crewman. "Let's get this thing off the ground. Activate communications and ask them if the mission should be aborted!"

The First Officer: "No, they said continue."

At first, I thought that we should incinerate the rest of them, but had a much better idea.

I asked the ship's doctor if she could save the crewmember and she said that fortunately the spear had missed his heart. In fact, it hadn't penetrated very deeply.

"How quickly will he recover? Will he be able to stand and walk?"

"He was almost killed! And you're asking that?" was her reply. "He's conscious and breathing. So far, I'm doing what I can to make him comfortable."

After about an hour, I asked him if he could continue performing his duties. He said that he could.

"Do you think you could return to the planet's surface and face the savages?"

"Yes, I think so, but why would we do that when they're proven to be hostile?"

"They might think that we're gods, after all. And we can leverage that to our advantage."

He was agreeable to my plan and donned his flight suit, the one with the hole and the bloodstain.

When we landed, the crowd gathered around the ship. When they saw my crewman, they threw down their weapons of spears and axes and fell prostrate on the ground. I felt that we were successful in introducing the subject of the existence of *deities* into their society. From that point on, they became quite docile, perhaps fearful. Therefore, the young females were easily corralled and herded onto the ship.

The doctor examined them to determine which ones were ovulating and began the inseminations. We released those females and kept the others onboard ship until they were ready for insemination. I told my First Officer that we'll release the other females to another tribe.

He responded by asking, "Would they be welcomed into another tribe?"

"What's the difference? They all look alike, anyway. I'm sure they'll blend in. By the way, do we have enough semen for another group of females?"

"Commander, we only have enough for three more."

"Well, tell them to *make* some more. Either that, or they'll have to physically mate with them."

"With those creatures? That would be disgusting!"

"I agree."

We finished inseminating the remaining females on board and proceeded to the next location; a sub-tropical climate in one of the southern continents. I asked our doctor, "What was their period of gestation?" She could only guess that it was the same as ours, perhaps a little longer.

We armed ourselves for the next encounter with the beings from this region. We'd learned from our mistakes with the previous tribe and were ready for the unexpected. The crewmember, who'd been injured, asked to remain on board. I acquiesced.

Curious regarding the new females introduced to their tribe, they gathered around them and somehow, communicated. They pointed at us and smiled. This was a positive beginning.

A male wearing some sort of a headdress, approached me. He was possibly their leader. I was correct about their appearance. They *did* look the same as the previous tribe, but they seemed to be more docile. Nevertheless, I ordered my crew to kill the leader and a couple of others to show our superior might.

They stepped away from the smoldering corpses, dropped their weapons and bowed down. Since the doctor was gentler in her behavior, I asked her to assist in guiding the females toward the ship.

The doctor observed: "They're petrified! Scared to death!"

"Wouldn't *you* be?" I answered.

We repeated what we'd done before and set course for the planet's northernmost continent.

"This area is very cold, so dress appropriately," I told them.

This tribe was also appropriately dressed, head to foot, in animal furs. Their leader, another male, approached us cautiously. I could find no other reason why they always walked toward me first, except that maybe it was because I was the tallest member of my crew. He looked me over twice, then turned and shouted something to his followers. They raised their weapons. So did we.

Before I had a chance to think about our situation, I could only rely on my intuition and gave the order: "Kill them all, but spare the females."

Unfortunately and collaterally, the females we wanted were also killed.

The rest of our mission went remarkably well with only a few minor incidences. And we were killing fewer of them. Yet, we continued to learn from our mistakes.

Our next encounter was in an arid region near the middle of their planet. Before we did anything else, we managed to separate the females. Then, we killed the rest of them. We discovered that they were slightly more advanced in their weaponry and had developed bows and arrows, which were just as deadly as spears, but could be shot from greater distances. I didn't expect one tribe to be more advanced than the others. I told the crew to be increasingly more vigilant.

I commended the male crewmembers for their perseverance with the production of much needed semen.

It had become our goal to eliminate the more aggressive males in the tribes we met as we continued to impregnate the primitive females.

At our next location, we were confronted with a tribe that as they circled around us, began to *salivate!* We sensed immediate danger and since they were too close for us to use our weapons, we ran back to the ship. Fortunately, they were too slow to catch us. With on-board weapons, we fired on them, leaving not one living thing within a twenty-five-mile radius. It turned out that we had annihilated *two* tribes.

The next tribe, from whom we had to run, were the most vile creatures of all. Though nearly hairless, they didn't bother clothing themselves. Instead, they adorned themselves with animal bones. In our haste to get away, it was discovered that one of us had accidently dropped a weapon.

The doctor's weapon was the one missing. I was forced to punish her by releasing her in the midst of the hairless natives. She protested, of course.

When we returned home from our mission, we were celebrated as heroes except for the actions I took on the day one of our weapons was left on the planet's surface. "Failure to supervise" was the charge. They did, however, say that the punishment I dealt to the doctor was appropriate. Nevertheless, they forced me into retirement without a pension.

It had been twenty years since our first mission to the primitive planet. Two ships were deployed to check on the progress of our efforts on that planet. This time, everything was on live-feed video. One ship reported that everything was progressing nicely, while the other ship didn't fare so well. It was attacked from the surface and destroyed in a holocaust.

I suspected our ship's doctor of instigating the destruction by abetting the savages, together with her offspring, in the development of the awesome weapon. I thought I'd keep silent about it for the rest of my life.

The government realized that there'd be no future colonization of that planet.

The Photograph

"All right, there are two matters to discuss before Monday night," the mayor intoned, clearing his crackling throat, "first the airport, second, the Centennial."

Councilman Mel Simmons spoke from the opposite end of the oak conference table. "The airport thing looks like it's a divided issue among the voters. Fifty-fifty. I say that we should move to put it on the ballot."

"You're absolutely right," Harvey McClanahan nodded, "that's what I was thinkin'. Opportunity's ours, gentlemen, all we've gotta do is take it. We'll propagandize the shit out of it ... tell 'em it's gonna benefit Cedar City and bring in tons of revenue. Okay? Everybody on board with this?"

I nodded, half-heartedly in agreement with the other four, from my lone position on one side of the rectangular table. Across from me sat Jack Peterson and Al Franzen. I had to agree. What good would it do to be adversarial? To be the only dissenter?

The airport would not be municipal or county-owned, but would be built and owned by the mega-corporation known as *Petro Technologies*. Their execs would fly in on their small jets from Miami, New York and Chicago and lay out the specs for a proposed site with enough acreage for an office building, a warehouse and a factory. And, not surprisingly, no one on this council will say anything to oppose them. Why should we when Petro will be generously lining our pockets? Each one of us, including myself, would expect a cash award if we pushed this through. Ethical standards were compromised that morning.

McClanahan looked at each of us and smiled. "Now, the Centennial. That's the last item for this work session, then we'll be done in time for lunch. The Centennial celebration begins in only three months. One of the things that'll happen is we're gonna dig up the time capsule that was buried in 1912 and put in a new one to be opened in 2112. It's goin' in the base of the new flag stand." We looked at each other and grinned like it was another fine idea.

"There'll be pictures, of course," the mayor went on, "news clippings and a copy of the city's web page. By the way, dress your best on Monday 'cause our secretary'll be takin' a picture of us."

I finally had to say something. "It's only October. Don't you think that we should wait 'til *after* the election? I mean, what if some of us don't get re-elected?"

The other three councilmen gave me astonished looks, as if I had said something heretical. Then, they shifted their gaze toward their leader for guidance.

The leader leaned forward and clapped the sides of his thin face in mock horror. He smirked and winked. "Mickey, me boyo, have ya no faith in y'self?"

Goddamnit, I hated whenever he did that phony accent. The only Irish thing about him was his name. In fact, he wasn't any more Irish than I am; mixed European like the rest of us.

"I haven't been called Mickey since the third grade. It's Mike."

He couldn't stand criticism and his mood changed abruptly from playfulness to solemnity. "Okay, Mike, then! Who's running for re-election?" McClanahan raised his hand. Al Franzen and I followed suit.

"And," the mayor added, "we *always* get re-elected. No opposition. There hasn't been a primary in ages. You're only goin' into your second term, Mike, and I've been elected and re-elected," he slapped his hands on the table and spread his arms, illustrating his point, "seven times and Al ... Al's been elected ... how many times?"

Al stared at me from across the table, then proudly stated, "Ten."

"Mel's too shy to say anything, but he's been here for six terms and Jack for three. See? You're just a rookie ... nothin' but a pup."

Maybe that's the trouble, I thought. Nobody can beat these guys, so nobody runs against them. And the voters, like sleeping sheep, cast their votes for familiar names.

One of the reasons why I won, is because there was a vacant seat left by old man Swenson when he died. The other reason could be my name, Mike Nelson; either because people thought it was a good, common Scandinavian name, or because my parents unwittingly named me after the Lloyd Bridges character in *Sea Hunt*, a TV show which reminded us that there was always crime in progress, even underwater. That's a thousand votes, right there, from the over seventy crowd.

And I didn't take offense at being called a "pup." After all, I was the youngest in this geriatric oligarchy. The next youngest was Jack Peterson and he was in his late fifties.

"Hey, Nelson," McClanahan broke my reverie, "I got an assignment for ya. Take the camera, go over to the library and snap a picture of Smith, the head librarian."

"Why me?"

"'Cause he used to be your high school teacher, plus you were always suckin' up ... cuttin' his grass and plowin' snow. He trusts you. Besides, he'd refuse to have any of *us* take his picture. You *know* he hates us. Petro wants their little airport right across the road from his house and he's pissed about it."

In lieu of a gavel, Harvey McClanahan banged his fist down on the table and declared, "Meeting adjourned."

The library was only three blocks away. I thought about walking, but drove over, instead. Black, torn clouds loomed on the horizon and I didn't want to walk back to city hall in the rain. I sat in my car for a while and thought about McClanahan. He owned an Irish pub called, *McClanahan's*, of course. It was the only Irish pub in Cedar City, more than likely in the county and probably in the entire western half of Iowa.

Every Saint Patrick's Day, patrons would gather around him, while he drank a couple of schooners of green beer and crooned, *Danny Boy* and *Galway Bay*. His singing voice wasn't that bad, but he'd begin in a baritone and felt that it was necessary to end songs on a high tenor note. Except his tenor was more like falsetto. People seemed to enjoy it, though.

I walked into the library with the camera strap dangling from my wrist. A teenage girl, an assistant librarian, sat at the main desk. "I'm Mike Nelson, here to see Mr. Smith."

"Mike!" Lowell Smith came charging out of his office. "I saw you drive up. Let's go back to the office and chat. What brings you here?"

Lowell was about six-feet four. The top of my head was level to the bridge of his nose. We shook hands when he noticed the camera.

"What's the camera for?"

"I've been asked to take a picture for the ..."

"Those crooks are having you do that for the stupid time capsule?"

Lowell Smith taught American History at Cedar City High School for about fifteen years. After his parents died, he inherited their house and a very large sum of money. He certainly didn't need a teaching job, or any other. His job as a librarian was strictly voluntary for which he accepted no remuneration.

"I don't want to have my picture taken! You may take a picture of my assistant, or the outside of the building, but not of me."

"Okay, I was just …"

"Step into my office. I want to show you something."

He placed a hand on my back and guided me to his small office. The first thing I noticed was the absence of bookshelves and, of course, books, but then again, he had an entire building full of books. A large metal desk stood against the wall, under the only window. Venetian blinds split the sunlight. The sun, I thought, would be blanketed in dark, gray clouds in less than an hour. Pushed in, at his desk, was an old-fashioned, wooden, swivel chair. I followed him into the room.

"Come in and shut the door."

His skinny frame made his clothes hang loose on him like a starving man. He was about my parents' age; mid-sixties. And he appeared to be in good health.

"Do you know why I returned to Cedar City?"

"Was it when your mom and dad passed away?"

"Yes. I was living in Des Moines, at the time …"

He momentarily drifted off topic.

"Well, when I received my due inheritance, instead of becoming a bum, I went to the University and earned a Bachelor's in Education, then came back here to teach twelfth grade. What year did you graduate?"

"2001."

"I began feeling quite disillusioned. Kids didn't seem interested in learning about things that preceded them. Only the here and now concerned them."

"But, *I* was interested."

"You were the exception, Mike. What did I give you for a final grade? Do you remember?"

"I think it was only a C plus."

"What if I had given you a B-minus? Would that have made you feel better?"

Before I could answer, even if I actually *had* an answer, he struck a teacher's pose; hands on hips and rocking back on his heels. He raised his eyebrows and looked down his narrow, pointed nose.

"The trouble with the grading system and all those pluses and minuses is that they're just an illusion. In fact, you could hardly slide a piece of tissue paper between two grades. It makes kids think that there really *is* a difference and who wouldn't rather have a B-minus instead of a C plus? How were your grades in college?"

"Mostly A's and B's."

"I had a feeling that you'd work harder in college. I'll get off that little diatribe, now. Come over here and look at this picture."

It was the only picture hanging on the wall in the square room; an eight-by-ten, black and white in a black frame. Lowell peered at it with his head tilted back, looking through his bifocals.

"You see these men? Scurrilous, all except one. The picture was taken at the front of the old schoolhouse. The grinning idiot, standing on the top step, wearing a derby, was going to be the mayor. He was also a banker. On the lower step, the owner of the *Mercantile Emporium* was going to be a councilman and the other councilman ran a haberdashery. Businessmen, except for this guy."

Lowell tapped his finger on the glass covering the photo.

"He was standing on the ground. Obviously quite a bit taller than the rest. That one was a farmer. He was wearing his 'Sunday-goin'-to-meetin' clothes. The sleeves on his black suitcoat are too short and his pants are, as well. See the black fedora he's cradling in the crook of his arm? And he's the only one not smiling."

I'd seen a copy of the picture in the archives at city hall. I looked at the picture and the farmer's expression was, indeed grim. He wasn't looking at the camera, but out of the corner of his eyes at something else.

"Except for the full beard, that farmer could be your twin, Lowell."

He dismissed my comment with a wave of his hand.

"Family resemblance. He was my paternal great-granddad."

"Really? I thought his name was Edward Schmidt, the bachelor farmer."

"If he was a bachelor, where the hell did *I* come from? He was a widower. Great-grandma died young. My grandparents changed the family name to Smith. Anyway, Great-granddad had owned a large chunk of farmland and the railroad was interested in coming through a half-mile swath of it. That would've decimated his corn crop. Mayor Wilkenson had planned to buy that part of the property and re-sell to the railroad at a profit. Old Schmidt didn't see any advantage to using the railroad to ship his crops, when he could just continue to drive them to market himself, so he refused to sell. Mike, read the caption at the bottom of the picture."

The names of the five men were printed in white ink and below the names, a date: September 4th, 1911.

"See that? September, 1911. The election wouldn't take place 'til November, for god's sake and they wouldn't assume office 'til March. They use to inaugurate in March, just like the big boys. *That's* how damn smug they were! Schmidt didn't even want to be in this picture. Do you know what he's looking at? He's looking toward his farm and worrying about getting his winter wheat planted, *not* getting his picture taken. The other four crooks had dreams of Cedar City becoming a boomtown and getting rich from it. What greedy fools!"

"So, what finally happened? I'd heard that some kind of terrible thing …"

"Yes, it did. To four of them, anyway. And all before they had a chance to take office. One of the council candidates committed suicide by way of a cavalry pistol. Another one was kicked in the head by a mule, the would-be mayor accidentally set fire to his office at the bank and perished. And the fourth was on his way to a tryst with his girlfriend in Storm Lake, when his car skidded off the road and into a tree."

"Your great-granddad survived the massacre?"

"Oh, yes. My parents and I visited him pretty often. Of course, I remember him as a very old man. He was ninety-eight when he died. Do you believe in history repeating itself?"

"Sort of. What do you think is going on?"

"This city government is similar to the one a hundred years ago. The railroad and now, the airport. I live in the same house in which Great-granddad lived and, I might add, I put a young fortune into remodeling it. After the war, my parents sold off parcel after parcel of that farm and left me with the original farmhouse and the last acre of land."

Lowell slumped into his swivel chair. I thought I saw tears welling up in his eyes. He put his elbows on the chair arms and tented his fingers, tapping them on his chin.

"The bank," I told him, "owns the land across the road from you and some acreage near the highway. They plan to give Petro Technologies a ninety-nine-year land lease. The issue will be on the ballot next month."

"Then it'll be done and they'll have their way. You can see that it's all about money."

"I don't see how it can be stopped."

He looked out the window at the darkening sky and gestured with his hand.

"Hell is empty and all the devils are here."

"Shakespeare?"

He rose from his chair and reassumed his teacher's pose. Then, he studied me for a moment and smiled.

"'*The Tempest; Act I, Scene 2*'. I think this is much more than coincidence. Do you know what else? Let's sit back and see what happens if you took your name off the ballot and didn't run again. I'm sure the furniture store will be glad to have you back full-time. Also, let's not leave anything to chance; don't let them take your picture for the time capsule ... please."

His eyes widened as if he were fearful of something, something tangible. He wore the same grim expression as that of his great-granddad.

I went back to my job selling furniture while the election went on. They found a replacement council candidate for me. The airport referendum was on the ballot and I voted, "No." The mayor, the original four councilmen and my replacement were decisively elected and the airport would be built. The execs at Petro had a good laugh, calling Cedar City, Iowa the "Gateway to the West." In the middle of November, chaos erupted.

Mayor McClanahan, in his zeal to get the airport built, flew to Chicago's Petro Technologies corporate headquarters. They evidently told him that they had changed their minds with regard to Cedar City and were subsequently looking at more suitable sites in North Dakota.

McClanahan returned home, disgraced, found a new rope and hanged himself in his garage. The newspaper ambiguously called his demise, "unexpected." Al Franzen suffered a fatal heart attack and the newspaper termed his death as, "sudden." Mel Simmons abdicated his intended throne and took off to North Dakota to find his fortune. The newspaper called his exit, "sudden and unexpected."

A hurriedly planned special election was slated for mid-December to fill the two vacancies. Jack Peterson, to celebrate his re-election and to enjoy a second honeymoon with his wife, Nadine, drove down to Tijuana. He stayed and she came back to Cedar City with signed divorce papers. Three vacancies.

My replacement, Veronica Erpelding, a twenty-seven-year-old, personal injury attorney, was ready to be sworn in on the third Tuesday in January.

The special election was held without a hitch. Erpelding was already on the ballot and the other three top vote-getters would head the city's government.

I had decided, with the aid of a substantial contribution from Lowell Smith, that I would run for mayor. I won easily.

The Centennial celebration had begun. The time capsule was buried, minus the photograph of the erstwhile mayor and city councilmen.

Out of the recent, reality shattering chaos, a new order of events materialized.

Trust

"**D**octor Voight?" Mrs. Bruner asked, as she timidly poked her head into Dr. Voight's small, but finely appointed office.

"Yes," the doctor answered and rose from behind a large mahogany desk, "you must be the Bruners. You're right on time. Please come in and sit down."

Mr. Bruner followed his wife and seated himself beside her in a black, leather upholstered chair. Dr. Voight took his place in a rocking chair near a Tiffany floor lamp.

"The head master," Mrs. Bruner began, "at our son's school, recommended that we come and see you about Wilfred's behavior. Wilfred ... our son."

"So, tell me about his behavior. Is he a bad boy?" The Bruners looked at each other quizzically. "Don't worry, everything that's discussed will remain in the strictest confidence. Go ahead, Mr. Bruner, did you want to say something?"

"Yes, well, our son is only sixteen and he thinks he should be independent of any and all rules. He *does* have his own money from an after-school job at a bookstore. I guess that's what makes him feel independent."

"Wilfred doesn't obey either of us!" interjected Mrs. Bruner, "but, he contributes some money toward household expenses."

"So far, he doesn't sound like such a bad boy, perhaps a little rebellious, but that's normal for his age; unless there's more ..."

"Oh, there *is*. Wilfred's already gone farther in school than me or my husband, but he doesn't appreciate it. He doesn't seem to want to continue. He hates studying and gets poor grades all the time ... can't focus on any of his school work."

Dr. Voight sat rocking, tapping his pencil on a notepad, passively looking at the Bruners and nodding his head. "Yes, please continue."

"I have to work nights at the Autowerks, right here in Stuttgart, so I really can't control him. He has no discipline. No discipline, whatsoever. He reports to work right after school; and after work he goes someplace and stays out late … comes home after his mother's gone to bed. He does this a few times a week."

"Well, do you have any idea where he goes?" Dr. Voight asked.

Mrs. Bruner: "Are you sure this is confidential?"

"Positively."

"We're pretty sure that Wilfred is involved with a group of kids who go to one of those *Swing Clubs* in Stuttgart. You know, it's where they listen to and dance to the most profane, American, Negro and Jewish music. Those clubs are illegal!"

"Yes, I know all about them and they *are* illegal."

Mrs. Bruner started to cry. "And that's not the worst of it. He goes there to meet his girlfriend. She's *Jewish!*"

"Now, that *is* an entirely different matter. Doesn't he know that even having a Jewish acquaintance is forbidden?"

Mr. Bruner: "Of course he knows, but we can't stop him. We're scared, doctor. We don't want the police, or the Gestapo to come knocking on our door in the middle of the night."

"Mrs. Bruner, how far along is Wilfred and the girl in their relationship?"

"What? What do you mean by that?"

"I mean, is it serious?"

"Oh, please don't ask that! I don't know and I don't *want* to know." She glanced at her husband for guidance, but he looked away.

"Now," Dr. Voight intoned, as he leaned toward the Bruners, "I want you to understand that I know how dangerous it is. For better or worse, Germany's changing. Hopefully, for the better, but let's concentrate on Wilfred. He, like all teenagers, is uncertain of the future and possibly fears what's happening in the world. It's become a very different world in 1937 than the one you remember. I assure you that it may be only a phase in which Wilfred is going through. Before you realize it, he'll be an adult and his rebellious nature will have withered away. I'm sure he'll turn out to be a fine, productive member of society. Well, I see that our time is up. I'd like to see Wilfred alone. I'll reserve some time next week for him."

"I don't know about this," protested Mr. Bruner, "we could barely afford to see you today and you say, 'send Wilfred.'"

"Look, Mr. Bruner," Dr. Voight said as he stood up and opened the door, "I've had to trim down my fees considerably these past couple of years and I've even had to let my secretary go *and* had to move to a smaller office. Since you've chosen me to be your family's psychiatrist, I'll continue by seeing Wilfred, gratis."

Mrs. Bruner hesitated, then asked, "Gratis?"

"Gratis. Free."

A week passed and Wilfred Bruner stopped in to see Dr. Voight. Wilfred scanned the wall and inspected each of Voight's framed university degrees.

"Are you interested in my education, Wilfred?"

"No, not really."

The doctor cleared his throat, "I'm just going to take a few notes and following our session, I'll lock them in my desk. Now let me ask you about your girlfriend. What's her name? I won't repeat it to anyone."

"If you don't repeat it. Her name is Ramona Kleinfeld. Why do you ask?"

"Your parents are concerned because she's Jewish and any relationship with a Jew, especially romantic, is forbidden by law."

Anger mounted as Wilfred, in a controlled whisper said, "It's forbidden by *Nazi* law and I don't agree with anything that's Nazi connected. Please understand, doctor, that I love Ramona. She's so much fun and she's gorgeous with thick, dark hair and light complexion. To kiss her is like taking a trip to heaven. I mean it! She's also teaching me all the hot, American dances! I just can't *live* without her!"

"You may *have* to live without her, Wilfred. It's much too dangerous for you. The police have already begun to raid Swing Clubs in some of the larger cities such as Munich, Berlin and Frankfort. If you get caught up in one of their sweeps, who knows? It's a good possibility that you'd be arrested ... maybe your parents, too! It'll be worse for you having a Jewish girlfriend!"

"I don't care! I won't give her up! I'll leave this stinking country and take Ramona with me. Maybe we'll go to America! So, go ahead, you Nazi headshrinker, turn us in to the Gestapo! I'm sure they'll pay you handsomely!"

"Will you keep your voice down? There may be people listening. We have to be careful these days."

"What? What did you say?"

"I said we have to be careful. Wilfred, I'm not a Nazi and I don't condone anything they do. I also believe that they're ruining Germany and want to ruin the rest of the world."

"I'm surprised you're telling me this. I thought you were on my parent's and my school's side."

"I'm on *your* side, Wilfred. I noticed that you speak in American colloquialisms and love American music. You even dress like an American. Perhaps, Wilfred, America is where you'd like to be. It's probably the safest place to be right now."

"I still don't understand, Dr. Voight. You sound like a heretic or something. Why, you're anti-Nazi after all. But, what can you do for me ... *and* Ramona? Can you help us? Will you help us get out of this miserable country?"

"I may be able to with help from other sources. I'd like to help Ramona, but I'm afraid that's not for me to decide. By the way, I'll let you in on a little secret—my name really isn't Voight. It's a good German name, don't you think? I changed it because I'm Jewish."

"This is incredible! You can actually help me escape! I'll warn you though. I'm not going if Ramona isn't included."

"I told you before. The Gestapo is everywhere and they're even getting suspicious of me. *I* may have to leave, also. It's just too risky to bring along a Jewish girl, but we'll try, all right? You may not be aware of this, Wilfred, but the Kleinfelds, her family, are well-known in Stuttgart for being subversive. Her father was a newspaper columnist whose inflammatory views caught the watchful eyes of the government censors and forced him to resign."

Ignoring the doctor's last comment, Wilfred asked, "When should we begin our plan? Next month?"

"No, next week. The sooner the better. You will not go to your job. Don't bring anything with you except for the clothes on your back. Tell Ramona to do the same. You will meet your contact, a man, in the bakery on Bergenstrasse, near city hall. Do you know the place?"

Wilfred nodded.

"You will walk to the pastry shelf and the contact will say, 'The pastries look good today.' You will reply, 'Yes, they do.' That's it.

That's the signal. Do you understand? I've already helped other people escape and have been successful every time. Don't ruin this or we'll all be killed. You only have this one chance.

"Your contact will drive you to the train depot where you'll board a train for Strasbourg, France. He will furnish you and Ramona with false Belgian passports. In the event that anyone asks, you are Belgian citizens, brother and sister, going home to your parents in Ostend, Belgium. Ostend is a seaport. You will wait for a Dutch steamship which will take you to New York City. Of course, you know enough not to tell anyone. *No one* must know, not even your parents. Don't leave a note or letter, either."

"Tell me something, Doctor, are you really a psychiatrist?"

"Yes, but I'm also M-5, British Intelligence."

"Fantastic!"

Wilfred ran to Ramona's school to meet her. Together they walked toward the bakery to meet their contact at exactly the appointed time and listened for the code words. They heard the words, "The pastries look good today" and turned around.

"Dr. Voight, what are *you* doing here?"

"It's been such fun that I thought I might as well be here myself ... just to see the looks on your faces."

The doctor's demeanor instantly changed to one of grave seriousness. His white goatee bristled as he raised his arm, signaling two other men who started walking toward them.

"I'm Dr. Voight of the Gestapo."

Deception

t the foot of the Carpathian Mountains, nestled among its rolling foothills, stood a rough-hewn cabin surrounded by a thick, dark forest.

It wasn't the cabin, but its inhabitants, Karl Chescu and his son, Anton, who were the focus of fear and concern among the citizens of the Village of Bistrita.

The mayor and the police chief sipped coffee at a sidewalk café. They met to discuss the growing problem with the old man and the boy who lived in the cabin.

"I say we force our way in and shoot the both of them," the chief insisted.

"But, we've never been able to prove anything," the mayor said.

"We know for a fact," the chief answered, "that they're Gypsies. Just look at them. They're dark, mysterious and foreign-looking."

"Look, chief, we'll go up there and find out for ourselves and you're *not* to bring your rifle. We'll only ask them some questions. That's all! Besides, I don't think they're Gypsies. The old man doesn't speak with a foreign accent and the boy doesn't speak at all. The poor thing's an idiot."

"I'm not going up there unarmed, Mayor. Might I bring my sword, at least? Or my dagger?"

"No sword. You may bring your dagger if you insist, but keep it concealed. We don't want to appear threatening. Is that understood?"

"Understood. I think we should bring the priest with us. We may need God's help."

"Get hold of yourself, man! Actually a priest isn't such a bad idea. We'll get the doctor to come along, as well. He's the smartest man in Bistrita ... university educated."

So, it was decided that a week from that day, the four leading citizens would confront the strange pair. They would meet at the edge of the forest, each on horseback and ride to the cabin.

The police chief, satisfied with the modest plan, leaned forward and whispered to the mayor. "I remember when this all started, my God, it must be twenty-five years ago. A lot of the farmers were complaining of missing livestock and some of our young people disappeared ..."

"Coincidental occurrences. Young people will leave our quiet village for the excitement of a big city. It happens all the time. They get on a train to places like Bucharest, to go to school or find employment."

"I know, I know but, I think you're wrong in minimizing this entire problem. I was a young policeman when I tracked the huge beast to the forest, right after it killed a half-dozen sheep and dragged their carcasses deeper into the woods. It was nighttime, and I had only the full-moon's light. I took aim with my rifle and shot the thing. It fell and cried a chilling howl and as I was reloading, it got up and ran, faster than before, toward the very cabin that we're going to visit next week. Now, of course, you probably think I'm touched, but I still believe that I had shot a werewolf."

The mayor laughed, but he wasn't entirely surprised at what he heard because he was well-aware of the infamous legend. "A werewolf?" he said, feigning surprise. "How do you know it was a werewolf?"

The chief answered, "Because it was larger than most wolves and it walked upright like a man. My eyesight was better when I was younger. It didn't betray me as much as it does now."

"It could've been a bear," the mayor said, as he dismissed the chief's statement with a wave of his hand. "The woods are full of them."

"Well, the old man walks with a cane, favoring the leg where I shot him. How do you explain *that*?"

"He walks with a cane because he's *old*, in fact older than we are. That's how I explain it."

"Anyway, after I shot him and for a few years after, some of the bravest townspeople took it upon themselves to ride into the forest and see the old man. They disappeared without a trace. *Without a trace!* Only their horses returned to the village. That's when the villagers asked me to organize another investigation. I know it's gotten worse this past year. Perhaps, nowadays he sends his son out to do his evil deeds."

"Maybe you're right chief, maybe not. One thing for sure though, is that we have to put a stop to it. That is, *if* they're the ones doing these horrific things. I've been told that the villagers live in terror every night. Especially when there's a full-moon."

The four men, the mayor, police chief, the doctor and the priest met as planned, at the trail leading into the forest.

"Gentlemen, it's about a half-hour ride to the cabin. Remember that we have to be out of the forest before sunset. Father, I want you to keep your fingers moving on your rosary beads. Doctor, are you ready? You can examine the old man's leg. A bullet mark, from when our policeman shot him, may still be visible."

"Mr. Mayor," the doctor said before they started out, "I realize that this is the Nineteenth Century and after all, we shouldn't still believe in creatures such as werewolves, but I have several medical books which say otherwise. Werewolfism, or in medical terms, *lycanthropy* may actually exist. Proving it, of course, is another matter."

"I for one," said the chief, glancing at the mayor, "am anxious to prove it."

"I pray it isn't true," remarked the priest, "if it is, may God have mercy!"

"**F**ather look," the young man said, as he peered through the window of the cabin, "there's some men on horseback."

"Are they coming fast or slow?"

"Slow."

"That's good, Anton. That's very good. They're probably going to conduct another of their foolish inquiries. It never amounts to anything."

"Then, why do they come?"

"Because you and I share a secret … an awful perversion. We are cursed with the same, evil affliction. The people of the village must never know what we really are. They would kill us without any further thought. So, when those men get here, be silent and pretend not to hear what we're talking about. I told them that you were a deaf-mute."

"Mr. Chescu, Karl Chescu," shouted the police chief, as he banged on the door of the cabin, "open up in the name of the law!"

"At ease," the mayor admonished, "we're not storming the gates like Prussian infantrymen!"

The robust old man hobbled over to unlatch the door and swung it wide open. With a bow and an arm gesture, he invited them in. Anton sat on the floor, facing the fireplace.

Karl almost laughed when the men stood there, shoulder-to-shoulder in front of the door. "Come in, come in gentlemen. To what do I owe the pleasure of this visit from such a noble group as yourselves?"

"This is not a social call, Mr. Chescu," the police chief began, "this is an official investigation. First of all, I want you to roll up your trouser and show the doctor your injured leg."

"And if I refuse?" Karl said, raising his eyebrows.

"Why then," the chief said stiffly, "I'll ... *we'll* have to take you into custody."

Karl sank into a chair and rolled up his right trouser leg to mid-thigh and then, slowly stood up, leaning heavily on his cane. The doctor mover in closer, adjusting his glasses, looking at Karl's leg from all possible angles. "No mark, no scar," the doctor proclaimed.

"May I roll down my trouser now? This leg is sensitive to the slightest chill. Rheumatism, you know."

The mayor asked, "Karl, how old is your boy, now?"

Karl turned and beamed at Anton, who sat motionless, still staring at the dying embers in the fireplace. "Anton will be twenty-two next month."

"Enough of this!" the chief announced, brusquely, "let's get out of here!"

"Then, you're satisfied, chief?" the mayor asked.

"For now, Mr. Mayor, for now." The chief said as he looked around the room, then opened the door.

"Please excuse this intrusion, Mr. Chescu. We'll be leaving now." The mayor added.

"The fools," Karl grumbled, "they didn't look high enough on my leg. I was shot in the hip, *not* the leg! And what's more, they were looking at the *wrong* leg! Now Anton, I want you to take the axe out of the closet and attack them just as you've done before. Circle around and charge into them with the sunset at your back."

"But, these are *important* men! Hundreds of villagers will come and ..."

"Nonsense, it *has* to be done. In about twenty minutes, you'll take Raven, our fastest horse and head them off, before they reach the edge of the forest. Then, Anton, give them the edge of the axe."

"Of course I will. Father, as long as I have a few minutes, could you tell me again about my mother?"

"Well," Karl replied, as he used a poker to stir the smoldering ashes in the fireplace, "she was the most beautiful woman in the village and fortunately, she didn't share our curse. You were only two when she died and I buried her at the base of the elm, nearest our home.

"You'd better go now, the sun's about to set."

"I have to ask you, Father, did you kill her?"

"Yes, but it was an accident. I'd changed into a werewolf. I frightened her. She came at me with a chair; screaming so loudly ..."

"It's all right, Father. You don't have to explain. What do you want me to do with their bodies?"

"Leave them for the bears, wolves and other scavengers of the forest. They'll feast tonight! Go, now."

Karl bent over to place more wood on the fire. Anton raised the axe and Karl, sensing motion, turned his head and, in a downward swipe, the axe sliced across the side of his neck severing one of his carotid arteries, spewing blood in every direction. The blow to Karl's neck, nearly decapitated him. Anton watched for a few minutes as his father lay quivering on the floor.

Anton realized what he had to do, what he *must* do. He mounted Raven and rode to meet the four visitors, telling them that he had killed his father and begged them to return to the cabin and see that the old werewolf was dead.

He dismounted, dropped to his knees and told the surprised men that he especially needed the priest's attention. He also desperately prayed to end his curse.

Anton's prayer was answered when he fell through the gallows trapdoor.

The Duck

When we were young, my brother and I had a pet duck to which we gave the obligatory name, "Donald." He was a huge, white creature that would run, flapping its wings at the neighbor's dog, scaring it away from the kibble it was eating. Then, the duck would eat the dog's food. I loved that duck. Sometimes I'd lay in the yard and use it for a pillow. He didn't mind at all.

He always stayed out in the yard because my dad wouldn't allow him in the house. One Sunday, as we were getting ready for church, I couldn't find Donald and asked my dad if he ran away. "No," he said, "he didn't run away. I gave him to a farmer. Winter's coming and he can't stay outside. You wouldn't want him to freeze to death, would you?" I didn't argue and that was that.

My older brother, who was about to enter his teens, didn't seem to mind that we'd never see Donald again. I guessed that he wasn't interested in semi-aquatic creatures anymore. But, the semi-aquatic creatures in which he became more interested, wore bikinis.

"Right after church," my mom announced, "we're invited over to Grandma and Grandpa's house for dinner."

We'd visit them quite often because they lived less than two blocks away. Donald would even stroll over there, once in a while. Grandma would feed him cookies. A couple of years later, we had a dog that would do the same thing.

Decades later, my dad made a confession; he didn't give Donald to a farmer. We ate him for dinner on that Sunday after church. We were told that it was chicken. He couldn't bear the thought of eating that duck, especially the way Donald gave one final look before my dad raised the hatchet and chopped his head off.

When he told me this horror story, my dad was in his late seventies and I reluctantly forgave him. On the other hand, when I phoned my brother and told him what happened so many years ago, he reacted like it occurred recently. He pitched a fit. "How could he do that? Only some kind of a Nazi monster would do something like that. I'll *never* forgive him!" Of course, we had other pets; a rabbit, a turtle, a squirrel, a robin and a dog. I wonder what became of them.

Rage

When those few people set out that morning, they had no idea that their lives would be cut short. Violently cut short. *Operation Desert Storm* had been over and done with for twenty years. Gerald Mason had served in the Army and was deployed to Kuwait during that conflict and came back home with PTSD.

Gerald had decided that in April, he'd deploy himself, along with his M-15A4B, to a foliated bluff overlooking I-35E, as it headed south into downtown Saint Paul. However, that April, winter had not yet removed its claws from what should have been spring. So, the travelers who had insisted on taking that freeway, would be benevolently spared ... temporarily. Gerald would patiently wait until June. This time of year would give him better cover. He wouldn't be wearing his desert cammies, so he had to buy some green ones at the Army-Navy surplus store.

He decided that rush hour was the wrong time. He'd observed their behavior during that time and concluded that people were driving too slowly even though a lot of them were nervously jockeying for position. *Didn't wanna be late for jobs they hate.* Gerald picked ten o'clock when they'd certainly be exceeding the maximum speed limit. *More sporting that way.* In a hurry going nowhere. Then, he could take his dutiful place as judge, jury and executioner. The job of a soldier.

He drove as close to what would be his hidden position and parked along the curb of a residential street. He had disassembled the M-15 so that it fit into a suitcase. Not to arouse anyone's suspicion. The hill was above street level, but the thick brush and tree line were perfect for concealment.

It reminded him of the *Highway of Death* in Kuwait when the Iraqi Army, most of them on foot, was in full retreat. Gerald was given the order to lay down fire behind them so that they'd move faster. Then suddenly, U.S. fighter jets began strafing the poor bastards. Presently, Corporal Gerald Mason's job was just the opposite.

He dropped onto his stomach and propped himself, making a tripod with his elbows, and tested the scope, for which he paid extra. Scanning the six lanes of concrete, the late drivers appeared to him as a herd of unthinking morons. But, in a hurry, of course.

Had to slow them down! Ah, an SUV in the passing lane which he undoubtedly thinks is the fast lane. Gerald ascertained that he would squeeze off a round slightly ahead of the vehicle in order to hit the driver. *Missed! He's going too fast! Have to fire behind him!* His shot went through the rear passenger window.

The vehicle jerked to the right, crossed the middle lane and was struck from behind and pinwheeled to the shoulder. Gerald peered through the scope and saw that the driver of the SUV was slumped against the side window. The car that hit the SUV, continued for about one-hundred yards before stopping. The driver exited on the driver's side. *Not smart.* It was a thin, young woman. He thought he would place a bullet through her thorax, when a pickup truck did the job for him. The pickup smeared her alongside of her car, also ripped off the door.

Isn't he gonna stop? Finally, he stopped on the shoulder. Gerald reserved the thorax shot for him, instead. That guy staggered into oncoming traffic and was struck multiple times. *This is turning out better than I thought.*

He continued firing at random vehicles. Sometimes at their tires causing them to spinout, or at the drivers and their passengers. He tried but failed to get that much-prized headshot. The sound of squealing tires seemed noisier that those of his semi-auto rifle. SUVs were his favorite targets, even when they didn't look like conceited, selfish, bullying assholes. Though, reasoned Gerald, most of them were. He gave himself the option to pick and choose, but changed his mind. He would exterminate as many as he could.

Gerald fired on anything that moved, or didn't. Those who didn't, were too terrified to move. *That's it! I'm a domestic terrorist! This'll make the national media. Maybe it'll be on CNN, MSNBC for sure!*

With all his shooting, he didn't hear the rotors of the approaching helicopter lashing the air. When the 'copter lowered and banked to its right, he felt the sudden storm of propwash.

He rolled over onto his back, bringing his rifle with him. He briefly glimpsed the passenger in the 'copter twist his body, aiming with a rifle of his own. *Too late to do anything.*

Oh, shit!

The Gift

he ringing phone and his wife's quiet conversation on it, was incorporated into a dream he was having. Marianne shook her husband's shoulder.

"Hank, wake up."

It wasn't a dream, he realized.

"You *have* to get up!"

"What? What's going on?"

"It's the nursing home. It's about Pops."

Their alarm clock was on Hank's side of the bed. He rubbed his eyes with a knuckle and stared at the clock. It stared back with red, digital numbers: *3:07 a.m.*

"What'd they say? Did they say to hurry?"

"No, but they said to 'come soon.' As soon as you can get there."

"Well, I think that means I'd better start heading up there. You can go back to sleep. I'll call you later with any news."

Of course, Hank knew what the news could be. Whenever the phone rings in the middle of the night, it's always either when someone's born, or when someone dies, or is about to die. And it's sometimes after a selfish night of drinking, debauchery and subsequent guilt. *Especially*, when one recalls what they were doing at the precise moment when a loved one has died. There was no such debauchery or drinking on that Friday evening in Hank and Marianne Whitfield's home and hardly any other evening. In fact they usually went to bed right after watching a talk show's host finish with his monologue and were not at all interested in the self-promotion of his celebrity guests.

"Do you feel debauched, Marianne?" Hank laughed.

"What the hell are you talking about?"

Hank's maternal grandfather, Pops, as everyone called him, was about to shuck-off the mortal coil which had been granted him, one-hundred-four years ago.

"Should I wear a light jacket?"

"Maybe, but it's supposed to warm up later."

It was Spring when everything comes back to life … and Pops lay dying.

"I'm gonna have to turn on the light, so close your eyes."

"Whatever you do," Marianne warned, "don't speed."

It was nearly two-hundred miles between where they lived and the nursing home. Pops' wife chose the place, because it was only a few blocks from where she, Pops and their children shared a home.

The state troopers would be on the lookout for Friday night revelers driving on the interstate. People going too fast, or too slow, for that matter, were usually pulled over. In either case, the cop's approach was the same. After one handed over the license and proof of insurance, the trooper would take off his big hat and stick his head in the car window, sniffing for telltale fumes of alcohol or weed.

Habitually, Hank set his cruise control to the maximum posted speed limit.

He didn't feel that there was time to shave, or brush his teeth, but made time to splash water on his face and run a comb through his thinning hair. There'd be time to stop for gas and coffee on the way.

"I'm going now," he said softly. Marianne was turned to the wall, asleep and didn't reply.

Past the city limits, he leveled his speed at seventy miles-per-hour. It began to rain. Mist fell onto the windshield. Hank Whitfield hated when it misted, because there wasn't even enough rain to use the intermittent wipers. They'd just rub and skip across the glass. Every two minutes, he'd have to manually engage the wipers.

Even though he had made the trip several times the past few months, he had finally begun to notice new housing developments and the inevitable, sprawling strip malls which hadn't been built that far out, ten, perhaps only five years ago.

It was Hank, Pops' eldest surviving relative who was selected by the family to deliver Pops' eulogy at his impending memorial service. This was about what he had been rehearsing and obsessing for the past few years.

One thing for certain, was that Hank's grandfather would be cremated. Pops had made it clear that he didn't care whether his remains were kept, or scattered someplace.

Despite having lived to the age of one-hundred four, Pops led a surprisingly unremarkable life.

He had been lucky enough not to have slogged through hell in two world wars, having been too young for the first and too old for the second.

His mother and father had emigrated from Austria when Pops was seven. When the immigration agent, filling out a ledger at Ellis Island, asked what the father's name was, the answer was a mumbled, "Heinrich Hopplemeyer." The agent, not having the slightest idea of how to spell it, shook his head and asked him what he did for work. Pops' father put a hand to his chest and replied proudly, "baker." The family name became *Baker* and Heinrich's first name was Anglicized to, *Henry*. In those days, Pops became known as Henry Baker, Jr.

There was nothing noteworthy in Pops' life except for maybe one thing: his two sons were younger than his great-grandchildren. He had married his third wife, seventy years his junior and fathered his two boys when he was in his early nineties. His first wife was Hank's grandmother. The second marriage produced no children. Pops had declared her a "lemon" and divorced her. He had outlived his first wife, as well as his first children. *Maybe*, thought Hank, *it* was *a remarkable life.*

Pops had been advised by his father, to rid himself of his accent. Any trace of a German accent wasn't too popular in America during, or after the Great War.

He left the job in his parents' bakery and traveled from New York to Detroit in 1925 to work for another Henry. Henry Ford. For two years, he worked on the line attaching rear bumpers to Model-T's and for the next four years, attaching rear bumpers to Model-A's.

Except for making two trips back to New York when his parents died, Pops remained in Detroit and his job until 1947. That was the year Henry Ford died and when Martha Firestone, Harvey's granddaughter, married Bill Ford, Sr., Henry Ford's grandson, it ensured that the empire would continue. In repeating the story, Pops would laugh and say, "That's what they used to do among the crowned heads of Europe."

With a few more miles to drive, Hank watched the eastern sky begin to lighten. Perched high in a grove of trees were a dozen or so, crows sitting silently, like courtroom jurors hearing testimony in a criminal case. When he drove by, they *all flew away to deliberate*, Hank imagined.

He brushed the thought away as he approached the nursing home's driveway and saw the sign: *Northview Healthcare Center.* He mumbled aloud, "Calling it a nursing home wasn't good enough. It had to be changed! Just like everything else!"

Just as if Ford Motor Company took too long to say, that too had to be changed to FoMoCo! And mortuaries became funeral homes. Hank supposed that sometime in the near future, they'd be referred to as, Aftercare Facilities.

Before he got out of his car, he saw an unbroken, lavender ribbon of cloud, stretching across the horizon, announcing the imminent arrival of the sun, which, by the way, was late, according to Hank. He smiled whenever he caught himself thinking like Pops.

He wiped the smile from his face as he approached the door. At this time of the morning, the place was dimly lit. Hank pressed a button adjacent to the aluminum-framed door, cupped his hands alongside his eyes and peered in through the glass. A stocky black woman came striding toward him from the long hallway, with a ring of silver-colored keys.

She came to the inside of the door, hesitated and spoke authoritatively, "Visiting hours are ..."

"I'm here to see Henry Baker. Someone called and told me to come."

"Oh, yes, Mr. Whitfield," she unlocked and opened the door, "come in."

When she opened the door, the distinct, acrid odor, a mixture of urine and excrement, with the underlying stink of vomit, hit Hank squarely in the face, sending his stomach into a slow somersault. He blinked his stinging eyes and stepped inside.

Fluorescent lights were encased in frosted, plastic panels. The acoustic ceiling tiles and the light panels looked as if they had been smeared with a thin coat of light brown water color. More likely stained from decades of cigarette smoke from an era when patients and staff were allowed to smoke at will. The dull, off-white linoleum (there wasn't a carpet in the entire place) was scuffed with black heel marks.

"I know where his room is," he said to the woman, as she trailed behind him.

Apprehensively, Hank walked down the silent hallway, past rooms of sleeping old people and perhaps, rooms of people who were already corpses. The woman, a member of the nursing staff, watched him enter Pops' room.

The bed nearest the door was occupied by a roommate, lying on his side, snoring softly. *Heavily sedated*, Hank thought.

"Pops, they told me you were ..."

Pops looked up from a book he was reading and cast his reading glasses aside, along with the book.

"Oh, hi kiddo," he rasped, in a thin whisper. "Yes I'm dying and so are you ... and so are we all. But, my time is today."

Hank yanked the curtain, separating the two beds, as far as the overhead track allowed. The noise made by the metal track didn't wake his semi-comatose roommate.

Pops' knees remained drawn up, under the white bedspread, as he had been using them as a bookstand. He was wearing his own pajamas; maroon with wide, yellow stripes. They added a little color to an otherwise drab room.

The pale skin on Pops' thin face looked too tightly stretched, revealing only traces of crisscrossed vertical and horizontal lines which were drawn downward and concluded in two crepey lines of wattle under his chin, running to his throat. At his temples, fingers of dark, blue veins, visible through paper-thin skin, flowed in tangled directions. Stubbles of white, wirey whiskers dotted his face and almost matched the sparse hair on his head, thanks to the buzzcut he was given a week prior. His dark, sunken eyes appeared startlingly bright, in contrast to his age-ravaged body.

He was still with the program. Pops' mind had outlived his body in a cruel trick of nature, when the incurable disease of old age takes hold. Sometimes, it works the other way.

Pretending to be astonished at how well he looked at one-hundred four (actually, Hank had no idea how people were supposed to look, past the age of eighty) "Pops, you don't appear to be dying. I mean, you look well enough to ..."

"You never *could* lie very well, kiddo. I know that a staff member called you and asked you to come. I know because I told her to call you."

Hank, in his early fifties, studied his oldest relative's face. *Was this how* he *was going to look when he was older? Nonsense!* He dismissed the thought as soon as it came to him. No one else in the family had lived much beyond seventy-five.

Pops, barely speaking above a whisper, "So, how's your family? Your wife and daughters?"

"They're fine. The oldest, Jennifer, recently moved to Indianapolis and the youngest, Susan, still lives in Madison with her husband and their three girls. They're well and happy, even though Jennifer's marriage didn't work out."

"And you, Hank?"

"I'm okay. Have Amanda and your boys been here?"

Amanda, Pops' wife, was about the same age as Hank's youngest daughter, a happenstance which was more of a curiosity to Hank, than a concern.

"They were here just before you arrived. Amanda might come back later without the boys. It's nice that we, I mean she, lives so close … it only takes her a few minutes to drive here. Now, enough of the pleasantries. Let's get down to business." He coughed a dry cough into the crook of his arm and continued, "As you know, I have a 'Will' and as much as I'd like to take care of everyone …"

"You've already taken care of my kids and me, sending us through college. Thanks, again."

"Don't interrupt! Let me finish! Of course, Amanda will get the house and the bulk of the money, with the rest held in trust as a college fund for my sons. That's it."

"That's fine. Say Pops, there's something I've always wanted to know … something that's been sketchy about your past. I mean, the amount of money you've made. Where did it come from? Ford didn't pay quite *that* well."

"Oh, he paid well enough, but it wasn't what I wanted. I wanted more. After I left Ford, I began with a string of sales jobs; shoes, clothing, furniture, real estate … I found that I could sell just about anything. All I had to do was look at people and they bought … bought things they didn't even need. Then, I gambled a little bit in the stock market. Gambling's what it really is, you know."

"It seems to me that you've led a charmed life."

"Luck, or you might call it 'charmed,' had absolutely nothing to do with it. It's the *Gift*.

"The gift?"

"Yes, kiddo, the Gift. My dad, as he was dying, passed the Gift on to me. The Gift *must* be passed on to one's oldest blood relative. In my case, that would be you."

"I really don't know what you're talking about. What kind of gift?"

"Kiddo, it's the gift of telepathy. I'm a telepath and I'm bestowing it on you instead of money."

"Frankly, I'd rather have money. Just a little joke there."

"Yes, very little."

"How do you propose to do it? How are you going to transfer this gift to me?"

"It's quite simple. But, we'll get to it. There's still time. First, I want to tell you what happened to me when I began to test my newly-found telepathy. I was walking around downtown Detroit, when I saw a man wearing a hat. I'd made eye contact with him and willed him to take off his hat and wipe the sweatband with his handkerchief. And, to my amazement, he did. But, it was a warm day and I chalked it up to coincidence. A while later, I made a woman look into her purse and search for money. Again, coincidence, I thought, when she boarded a streetcar. But, they *weren't* mere coincidences.

"I started to have fun with it, kiddo. I made people, men and women, start scratching their asses and crotches in public, light cigarettes and then, stomp them out right away, bend over and touch their toes. Silly things like that. But, then I started using the Gift more seriously. Somewhat more seriously. I found out that telepathy didn't work unless I made full eye contact. So, I couldn't do it from a distance. I wished I could, though. I had gone to a racetrack and found out that it didn't work on horses, either. One day, while I was working at the Ford plant, Ford himself, came to inspect the line. I made eye contact with him and mentally suggested a new design. He must've had, what he thought was an epiphany and believed that he had developed the design for the Model-A, all by himself. Do you get it now, kiddo? I made most of my money in sales … a small fortune, in fact. See, telepathy works on everyone except children and other telepaths. Did I mention horses?"

Hank grinned, "What am I thinking now, Pops?"

"I don't have to read your mind because I already know what you're thinking. But, I can't read minds. By some strange twist, I can only use the gift one way. In other words, I can only transmit, I can't receive. I can tell from your expression that you're skeptical."

89

"Well, I *am*."

"Okay, then. I'm thinking of my family's first dog. I'm the only one who knows this. What was its name?"

"It was a female and her name was, 'Hildie.' She was a yellow lab."

"That's right! You didn't have to guess. Are you convinced?"

"Almost."

"It was at my seventieth birthday party, the last one I'd ever allow ... god, I *hate* those things ... strangest human ritual there is; celebrating another year closer to death. Then comes 'Happy Deathday' ... let's celebrate! Sorry, I'll get to the point. You were at my party and we had been having a conversation about your going to law school, when you abruptly told me that you'd changed your mind. Remember?"

"Yes, I vaguely recall."

"You went on to tell me that you were going to change your major course work to English and that you wanted to teach it. Now, tell me, do you think that was your *own* idea?"

"I thought it was. Wait a minute ... are you saying that it was your ... that you planted the idea?"

"Yes, it was. What do you do for a living, now? You went on to get your Master's in Education and you're an English professor at the University. Right, kiddo? I thought perhaps you'd like instructing much better than prosecuting or defending."

Hank was more sincere, when he said, "You were right all along. Thank you."

"Let's do the transference now. My time is running short."

"How do you know you're going to die soon?"

"Oftentimes, people have the uncanny ability to see it coming, kiddo, and they simply want to let go. So, please," Pops patted the side of the bed, "sit down."

Hank sank down on the bed and wondered if he was doing this to humor the old man, or that he truly wanted to do this. *Maybe*, he thought, *I really want to do this.*

They locked eyes and Hank began to read Pops' thoughts: *Kiddo, you will promise to pass the Gift to your oldest daughter.* Hank nodded. Pops' mouth wasn't moving. *It was*, Hank thought, *quite amazing!*

Pops suddenly grabbed Hank's right wrist, with a bony, liver-spotted left hand. His right hand clapped behind Hank's neck. What he thought would be cold hands, he found that they were actually very hot and tried to pull away, but couldn't move. Then, the pain, a terrific and terrifying pain began to build inside his brain, from the center, radiating outward. There were acute lightning-like flashes, so intense, so bright that Hank could understand how migraine sufferers felt when they were under attack.

He thought, then yelled it through clenched teeth, "For chrissakes, Pops, stop it! I can't take it anymore! I feel like I'm dying!"

You're not dying, Pops thought, soothingly, *everything's going to be all right. You're all right. It's almost over. Be patient.*

Hank winced against the pain. Tears streamed down his cheeks. Or, was it blood? His eyes bulged, and the room seemed on fire. Thin snot poured from his nostrils. Or, was it blood? Certainly, the coppery, familiar taste in the back of his throat *had* to be blood!

Pops' lips were tightly pressed together, the corners of his mouth turned down. Then, his lips parted, into a grimace, across an even row of dentures.

Just think, kiddo, you'll acquire more memories ... down through our generations of ancestors ...back to the beginning ... back to our origins in East Africa ... their travels North ... melded together. And finally, my memories. Everything I've seen and done ... everything I know, will become part of your memories.

At that moment, Pops loosened his grip. Hank opened his eyes and with one hand behind Pops' head, eased him back into a lying position. His jaw slackened and with half-lidded, unseeing eyes, stared at the acoustic ceiling tiles. *He's dead,* Hank thought, *no doubt about it.* And as he pushed the nurse's call button, Hank whispered to himself, "Thanks a lot, kiddo. So long, Hank Whitfield. Hello, Henry Baker, Jr."

The Witness

Where were you last night? Were you home in bed, or were you out sampling the night life downtown, in the city you've always called home? If you were home in bed, as perhaps you should've been, you wouldn't have witnessed a woman killing a man in an alley behind the nightclub. You wouldn't have seen the knife glinting in the dim light of the lone street light. You wouldn't have seen her make the upward plunge of the blade under his rib cage, into his side and you wouldn't have heard the scraping sound of the knife's serrated, steel blade against bone, as she dragged the knife back out. You wouldn't have seen her finish him off with a backhand slash across his throat. But, you were there.

She noticed you, out of the corner of her crazed eye and turned to face you. You were standing, mouth agape, only about twenty feet away. With the knife still in her hand, she was breathing hard, as the large man slumped forward to the dirty pavement.

She got a *very* good look at you and started toward you. You back peddled, then turned to break into a full sprint. You thought about running to your car which was a half-block away, but you reasoned, it would take too much time to unlock the door, put the key into the ignition and start it. So, you ran.

Whenever you saw a crowd of people on the street corner, you ran toward them. You had to run past them because there wasn't enough time to explain to anyone why a woman was chasing you and what you had witnessed. You ran. That's all you could think of. You ran until you thought your heart would explode.

Finally, after you'd run a couple of blocks and backtracked through an alley, you looked back to see if she was running behind. She wasn't. After, what seemed like forever, you caught your breath and stumbled back to your car.

You drove to the nearest police station. You *had* to tell them what you'd witnessed. Still shaken, but greatly relieved that you made it safely to the police parking lot. You thought that a police station parking lot was the safest place to be, besides being *inside* a police station.

You opened your car door and set foot on the asphalt, when suddenly, the woman who'd been chasing you was standing just outside your driver's side door. You recoiled in terror, gasping loudly and clapped your hand over your mouth to stifle the release of a scream. A muffled cry came out anyway.

"Slide over," she whispered, "we're going for a little ride." You obeyed and slid over to the passenger seat.

Stunned, you asked her how she got there ahead of you and why she was there at all. Calmly, she put the car in gear. You heard her mention that she was going to drive around the block a few times and explain some things. Though you had to be careful of what you said, you blurted, "Do you *always* go around killing people and act so nonchalant about it"

"It's *only* business," she replied.

After a long silence, you spoke: "What are you, CIA? The Mafia?"

She smirked and answered, "I wouldn't tell you if I *was*. What I *will* tell you is that man you *think* you saw me kill, was one of many enemies ... the worst of his kind."

"Who was he then, your husband?" You joked.

"No," she said flatly, "he, uh, works for the same company," her voice trailed off.

"I suppose," you said, "you're one of the good guys and that you're the best of your kind."

She emphasized that she was just doing her job and added, "What else could I have done? He was trying to kill me, too! Do you think that the wrong person was killed?"

You mumbled, "No."

Without your asking, she told you that she had arrived at the police station shortly before you did and she guessed that you would come there, as well.

"I identified myself to the police and reported what had happened," she casually told you, "and that they had to go out and scoop up a 'John Doe.' I also told them that if a man came running into the station to report an alleged murder, they were to calm him down and tell him that he misinterpreted what had happened. No one had actually been killed. By meeting you in the parking lot, like I did, I saved you the embarrassment of talking to the police."

"I don't get it," you said, "why are you telling me all this? Why don't you just kill me and get it over with?"

She smiled and said, "Because you're not my type." She pulled your car back into the police parking lot and gave you a chilling admonishment: "Remember always, that what you saw, never happened. You will never tell anyone; not even your mother, or closest confidant. If you do, I'll find you."

You then made a foolish comment: "You don't know who I am, or where I live."

She gave a mocking laugh and informed you, while tapping on your steering column, "Everything I want to know, is right here on your vehicle registration."

You shuddered.

"Now," she advised, "go home and forget all about what occurred tonight, and, by the way, you never saw me, either."

You nodded. She waited near your car, until you drove away, watching your taillights as they disappeared into the darkness.

You went home, took some sleeping pills with a glass of Seagram's and went to bed.

Last Evening

"**A**nd now, the Evening News with Kathy Conway."

"Good evening. First, some really bad news ... I mean, I hate to be an alarmist, but there are reports coming in now, which would suggest that the world is coming to an end. With more on the story, we switch you to our senior science correspondent in Washington, Jules McNamara."

"Yes, Kathy, by some freak accident, the Earth is apparently free-floating in space, away from the sun, after a gigantic, meteor, or asteroid struck near the outskirts of Moscow at about 7 a.m., Eastern Standard Time."

"Jules, does anyone know why it wasn't seen with a telescope?"

"That's an excellent question. It wasn't seen because it's a dark mass which, oddly enough, left no fiery tail, as most meteors and comets do. In addition, reports coming from Moscow say that the object is nearly the size of Alaska and when it struck, the force of which caused the Earth to be bumped out of orbit, away from the sun."

"So, it's *that* serious, Jules?"

"Yes, *very* serious. In fact, the Earth is no longer turning."

"Is that why it looks as if it's been noon all day?"

"Yes, when it struck, we moved about a half-turn and that's it. It's never going to turn again."

"Jules, it started to feel colder by the minute, even under the studio lights, I had to put on a winter coat."

"In a day, or maybe just a few hours, we won't be able to see the sun and we won't be thinking about how cold it's getting, either. We won't even be *thinking*. It will mean the end of civilization and the end of all human history."

"And all the good people will perish?"

"Yes, the good, along with the bad."

"Do you think that sometime, in the future, an alien civilization will come along and discover this planet?"

"How the hell am I supposed to know, Kathy? Besides, all they'd find is a frozen rock."

"Jules, have we learned anything from all this? Is there anything which could've prevented this from happening?"

"Absolutely nothing could've prevented this, except if we had destroyed ourselves with a nuclear war, first. The one thing, the only bright spot, is that we'll all freeze to death very quickly."

"It's still too bad though, with elections coming up and everything."

"Kathy, a note just got handed to me … the president, his family, cabinet members and a few friends, took off moments ago, aboard Air Force One, heading, in what they believe is a westerly direction. Actually, they're heading east."

"But, Jules, isn't that the wrong direction since the planet turned?"

"Yes, and they'll be the first to freeze to death."

"Jules, since this may be … since this *will* be our last broadcast, let me say this to you; I've always found your reports interesting, but you have such an arrogant demeanor, that it makes me nauseous."

"And Kathy, I wish that I could say the same to you, but I can't. Instead, I'll tell you that I could never stand your flippant treatment of news stories, even hard news items. You always seem to give them a healthy dose of insipience."

"Thank you, Jules McNamara. And now, we take you to Moscow and our roving correspondent, Arthur Nelson. Arthur, are you there?"

"Of course, I'm here Kathy. I apologize for using a cell phone. Our satellite feed froze up and we lost the signal."

"How are things, there?"

"Pretty chaotic. People are pushing and shoving, trying to get closer to the crater for a little bit of warmth. But, from my vantage point, the object seems to be cooling off. People have been tossing things into the crater; items that will burn slowly, such as livestock and household pets. A man had to be restrained from throwing a ten-gallon can of gasoline into the pit, which would've caused an explosion and injuries. Not that it would've mattered very much."

"Arthur, how are *you* holding up?"

"Thanks for your concern, Kathy, but I'm not doing well, at all. I can't move because of the apparent onset of hypothermia. Only my upper torso seems to be freezing more slowly. That's possibly due to these kind people continually pouring vodka down my throat."

"Arthur, Arthur … oh my, we've lost contact. Well, that was Arthur Nelson reporting live from Moscow.

"Ladies and gentlemen, I've just been told that parts of the northwest are buried under seven feet of ice. The actual temperature has been recorded at minus sixty-five and dropping. Rescue efforts had to be abandoned because the rescuers, themselves, froze instantaneously.

"I'm also told that none of it matters, anyway. And no one's watching this broadcast. Is that right, guys? Guys? Jules, you son of a bitch, you miscalculated the rate of speed we're traveling away from the sun! I'm getting drowsy and starting to freeze up. I can't even finish the newscast!

"This is Kathy Conway, signing off. Before I do, I'd like to quote the esteemed, immortal journalist, Edward R. Murrow, 'Good night and good luck.'"

Stalker

Following his wife's death, Jerry found that moving to a one-bedroom apartment was quite adequate for himself. Actually, more than adequate since her sizeable, life insurance policy paid off. He was able to finally retire from his job as an English teacher at Adams Middle School. Besides, he was tired of trying to teach, to whom he'd often refer as, "those imbecilic, little shitheads" and added that, "English to them, seemed to be a foreign tongue."

Jerry Montague took his beer out onto the balcony to enjoy the sunset on a cool, mid-September evening. He had to don a sweater. One wasn't sure how to dress this time of year, when daytime temperatures were warm and the evenings cool.

Across the alley, he had an unobstructed view of the neighbor's backyard and had the opportunity to observe their peculiar habits. One of which was, during the waning baseball season, he'd see Eddie waddle out to his detached garage to watch the game on TV. He had all the comforts of home in there: TV, chaise lounge and a liquor supply. Jerry had concluded that Eddie's wife didn't like baseball, but perhaps it was his cigar smoking, or the fact that he was a balding, sweating, heap of corpulence that drove him from the house and into the garage. All the neighbors knew he was watching the game, because he'd open the door and the play-by-play could be heard, along with him cheering … or, booing.

The hometown team wasn't in contention for the playoffs that year and that fact became evident soon after the All-Star break. So, personally, Jerry had lost interest.

Earlier in the spring, he had enjoyed watching Eddie's wife in her garden, weeding, planting flowers and vegetables. Eddie was about Jerry's age; fifty years old and she was, from the looks of her, at least ten years his junior. She'd come out of the house with her gardening tools, wearing a sun visor and sunglasses, a white tank top and, most noticeably, tight short-shorts, also white and quite thin … so thin, that from his vantage point, he could discern panty lines. Her tanned complexion was accentuated by the white clothing. Her hair, a light brown, was done up in a ponytail. She had a body too good for Eddie.

With her back to Jerry, she knelt doing her work while he stared at the two, perfect, pear-shaped globes of her ass. She crossed her ankles and would occasionally sit back on them and admire what she'd done, while he admired her.

It was on that particular fall evening, Eddie didn't stagger back into his house, as he usually did when the game finished. Jerry had assumed that his wife, whenever he didn't return to the house, for whatever reason, instinctively went out to check on him. Then, that evening, an ambulance pulled up in the alley alongside their garage.

The next morning, Jerry Montague went over to their house and asked what had happened. She appeared at the door wearing jeans and a tube-top and told him that Eddie had suffered a heart attack and died on the way to the hospital. He wanted to articulate his condolences properly, but "I'm very sorry for your loss," came stumbling out instead.

She said, "Thank you," smiled weakly and invited him into the kitchen for coffee. She introduced herself as, Linda. He told her his name was Jerry and said that under different circumstances, meeting her would've been a pleasure. She nodded and turned away. Linda's eyes looked red-rimmed and puffy, *likely*, imagined Jerry, *from crying all night*.

He held her hand in both of his and said, with practiced sincerity, "If there's anything, anything at all, that I may do for you, all you need is to ask."

She took two coffee mugs, placed them on the table and motioned for him to sit down. To make room, she slid a stack of unopened mail to the edge of the table and placed a half-scissors on top. Linda caught him staring quizzically at the scissors.

She smiled, "Oh, the scissors … they broke apart. I use it for a letter opener, not much good for anything else. Cream and sugar?"

He shook his head, "No, thanks. Plain is fine."

"I was in the ambulance when he died." Black rivers of mascara ran down from the corners of her eyes. She plucked a napkin from a holder and carefully dabbed at the tears. "He was only fifty-two. I don't know if it was because he was overweight, or his drinking, or those awful cigars …"

"Maybe," he offered, "it was a combination of all those things."

"I think you're right, Jerry. I just don't know."

"It's none of my business, but is an autopsy planned?"

"No. That wouldn't do any good."

"I know, but ..."

Jerry didn't say anything like, "I know how you feel." Instead, he lied, telling her that he'd been divorced for several years and didn't have any children. He didn't want to tell her that his wife was dead and that he aided in her demise. Prescription sedatives, plus the fact that she was an alcoholic seemed, to any reasonable person, to add up.

Linda, then confided in him that she and Eddie neither had any children, nor had a satisfactory relationship. He was not entirely surprised, having seen Eddie.

She mentioned her sales job at the jewelry store and that they'd given her an emergency leave of five days and Eddie's funeral would be in three days. He'd be paying for it himself from the insurance money.

The reviewal or wake, took place the evening before the funeral. Jerry attended, wearing his black suit. Attendance was sparse, and Linda was standing, also wearing black, near the open casket. She appeared to be unemotional and her eyes were vacant, staring off somewhere. Jerry walked up to Linda and stood in front of her, stretched out his arms for a brief embrace, but when he deliberately let his hand slip down to the small of her back, she pushed him back, her eyes flashed. He shrugged, feigning innocence. He worried that she was angry with him.

The next day, at noon, was the funeral. This time, he wore his charcoal gray suit. While the priest droned on with Eddie's eulogy, a preposterous one at that, Jerry stared at Linda's profile. She wasn't dabbing away tears, as he had expected, but was passively listening.

After the trip to a nearby cemetery, there was a buffet-style luncheon in the church basement. It was setup with several round tables. A few of Eddie's relatives sat with Linda and Jerry sat alone. Many tables stood empty. The event was definitely not a sell-out.

After the luncheon, he was walking to his car. Linda tapped him on the shoulder.

"Jerry, I didn't want to appear stand-offish, but you know what it'd look like. I didn't want to look *too* friendly, so soon.

"Oh, I understand."

"Do you want to come over for dinner, sometime?"

"I'd be delighted, Linda."

"Okay. How about this Sunday, then?"

She made mashed potatoes, but the chicken and coleslaw came from the deli at the supermarket. After dinner, he invited her to a movie. "Next week," he said. He didn't want to rush things. She agreed.

They had several dates before November … before the sky turned battleship gray and the snow began to fly.

And when the snow, in the inevitable surrender of fall to winter, began to accumulate in earnest, he used Eddie's old snowblower to plow her walks and driveway. Every weekend and some weeknights, they continued dating. The dates had been platonic and according to Jerry, that *had* to change.

On one particularly cold weekend, they had dinner, followed by a movie.

"I know a place, Linda, where we can sit and view the cityscape. They've already begun to put up Christmas decorations on some of the buildings."

"Where is this place?"

"You might've been there. It's the park on the hill near the cemetery."

She hesitated. "I don't know. That's the cemetery where Eddie's buried. Remember? That would feel kinda creepy."

Kinda creepy? He thought. It was odd hearing a woman in her forties saying a word like, "creepy."

"Nonsense," he told her, "there's nothing creepy about it. The dead aren't going to bother you."

Linda smirked, "I guess that *did* sound a little immature. Okay, you're on. Let's go, then."

They drove to a parking lot on top of the hill and the view was breathtaking. The lights of downtown shimmered in the clear, still night. Smoke and steam rose in columns, from the skyscrapers, eerily backlit from the light of a half-moon.

"Are you cold?" She nodded. "I'll keep the car running, then. Do you think we'd be more comfortable if we moved to the back seat?"

"What? What the hell for? Are you nuts?"

He realized, then and there, that he'd have to make his move.

"Just relax, will you?" He unfastened his seatbelt and reached over to unfasten hers.

"What do you think you're doing, Jerry?"

"What do you *think* I'm doing? I think it's about time we get better acquainted."

"I don't like this! You're scaring me! Take me home right now!"

He placed one hand on her thigh and the other on her shoulder. Linda's face turned pallid, almost instantly, as the color drained away. Even in the dim light, Jerry could see her lips turning white.

She grasped the door handle and Jerry batted her hand away. Her eyes widened, as she drew a deep breath.

"Hey, don't even think about screaming … no one will hear you anyway. Besides, I wouldn't like it. I don't want to have to hurt you! I really don't."

She began to scream, starting thinly, then building to a throatier crescendo.

"I *told* you not to do that!" he growled. Quickly, his hands reached for her neck and, just as quickly, she reached into her purse and felt for her nail file. With one sidearm motion, she thrust the file into the side of Jerry's neck and sunk it in, as far as she could.

His hands fell from her neck and reached for his own, frantically feeling for the file. This time, *his* eyes were wild with fear, as he yanked the file out of his wound; now gushing an even tempo in torrents of blood over both of them and the car's interior. The nail file clacked against the windshield, leaving a dark smear and fell to the dashboard. He grabbed his neck in a futile attempt to stem the flow pumping between his fingers.

Linda let out a high-pitched laugh, as she watched his face turn from the look of shock, to one of sheer terror. His mouth opened wide, appearing as if it was coming unhinged. His lips twisted and curled against his teeth. Jerry was struggling to say something, but instead, a sound rose up in a thick, sickening gurgle. He coughed. A fine spray of blood flew from his mouth.

"Eddie got what he deserved. I spiked his booze with enough sleeping pills to kill an elephant and now, you stupid bastard, you're getting what *you* deserve."

As Jerry started to slump toward her, his eyes staring, but not seeing, she scooped up her nail file and backed out of the car. "Thanks, Mr. Montague ... had a wonderful time. I think I can walk home from here."

The Compromise

The previous night, there was a brief, but fierce battle in the clearing of a wooded area.

What had become an all-too-common sight, following a battle, was the appearance of wagons to haul away the dead. A ceasefire was ordered for both sides and I watched, from a distance, as the enemy's wagon made its way toward the bodies. The screech of the wheels and the moans coming from the wounded, emitted an eerie lament.

Small groups consisting of two soldiers, grabbed the arms and legs of the dead and solemnly, but unceremoniously hoisted them into the wagon, double-stacking them. A wagon came for our boys too, though we didn't have as many dead.

The following morning, just before sunrise, I was selected to do some reconnaissance and hike about two miles north of where our battle took place, to try to determine if the enemy was planning to regroup and attack once more.

It was a nice, warm, spring morning. A low mist hugged the ground which usually meant that as soon as the sun rose, it was going to get unbearably hot and muggy.

I stopped to rest near a clearing in the woods and sat down in the tall grass. I cradled my rifle in my arms, drew out my pipe and packed it with tobacco that had turned dry. It burned so fast, that I only got about three puffs and it was gone.

Suddenly, there was a man carrying a rifle, cautiously winding his way through the woods. I rolled onto my stomach and squinted through the sights of my rifle. As soon as he cleared the woods, I squeezed the trigger. The acute noise sent birds flying in all directions. The flapping of their wings sounded strangely like an appreciative applause erupting from a theater audience.

I got him in the right leg! He pirouetted on his left and fell; the mist rushed away. His rifle fired harmlessly into the air. As I reloaded, I watched him crawl toward a huge oak tree which was wide enough to conceal him. I crept as silently as I could behind the tree.

"Throw the Enfield out where I can see it."

"But, it's not loaded."

"Mine is, Johnny, and I've got a good mind to come around this tree and send a mini-ball into your brainpan."

He flung his rifle out and I walked around to see a young man sitting and leaning against the tree. He had blond hair and blue, frightened eyes. His youthful appearance and what seemed like an attempt to grow a full beard, albeit a wispy one, prompted me to ask his age.

"How old are you, Johnny Reb?"

"Eighteen."

"You look more like fifteen. Goddam Bobby Lee'll send *kids* into hell! Where you from?"

"'Lanta. 'Lanta, Georgia."

"Lemme look at that leg."

"It hurts somethin' awful! I can't walk! Why'd ya have to shoot me, you Yankee bastard?"

"Why do you think? 'Cause you're the enemy, that's why. Anyway, what're you doin' here?"

"I'm not gonna tell you."

I took my bayonet, cut his pant leg and wiped away some of the blood.

"Hey, it's not so bad. The ball passed through your skinny leg, just above the knee. I thought that you might have to have it amputated. I'll make a bandage from your bedroll. Where's your company? Are they planning anything?"

"I don't know."

"They'll probably come looking for you, so I'd better go."

"You can't leave me! If they find me, they'll kill me! I'd be better off if you take me prisoner!"

"Why?"

"'Cause I'm a deserter. A few of us escaped during the night, heading in different directions."

"Well, where do you think you were going?"

"Home. I was plannin' on walkin' home."

"To Atlanta? That's about fifty miles!"

"I could've made it, but *you* had to shoot me."

"Listen, boy, I'll take you back to my camp. Our Doc'll look at your leg and you'll probably spend a few days in the infirmary tent. Use your rifle as a crutch and lean on me."

"Are you gonna tell 'em I'm a deserter?"

"Nope, I won't say anything to anybody. As far as anyone's concerned, you're only my prisoner. Our commanding officer'll ask you where the rest of your company is and of course, you'll be obliged to tell him."

"Yes, if I must. I might also tell him that the war's almost over for us."

"I agree. It'll be over in a few weeks, maybe a month. It'll be when Lee gives up, sees the blood on his hands and finally realizes the futility of continuing."

"It'll be over when Lincoln decides and General Lee agrees."

"What do you mean by … did you hear that?"

"Hear what?"

My prisoner turned to look over his shoulder and I noticed his lips part in a wry smile. I looked behind us and saw some figures in the woods, moving around and crouching.

"I don't know what you're up to, Reb. I should shoot you dead, right now."

"Whad'ya mean?"

"I saw you kinda smiling.' What's goin' on? Is this a trap?"

Then, the enemy opened fire. I must've heard ten rifles go off at the same time; their rounds tore through the leaves and branches. Some of the lead hit the trees with a thunk. I grabbed ahold of the boy-soldier and hid behind a large tree to reload.

"We gotta get outta here! You know, they could kill you, too! I don't care much about you, but both of us hafta run as fast as we can!"

I made him run ahead of me. Even though he dragged his wounded leg, I encouraged him to run faster. Even when I was sure we were out of range, I turned and shot back.

We both made it back to camp and told the Captain about the ambush and that the Doc should look at the Reb's leg.

"I've got a better idea, Corporal," the Captain said, looking through a spyglass toward the woods, "change coats with him and we'll send him out with a white flag."

109

"But, they'll think he's one of us and shoot him."

"That's the idea. You're getting smarter by the minute."

The Captain called for the four artillery units to move forward. He then ordered fifteen of our best sharpshooters to flank the enemy from the right and take cover. Of course it would draw their fire, distracting them.

"How many of them are there, Corporal?"

"Only a few of 'em. I'd say about twenty."

"Watch what happens when the Reb walks out there."

The Reb bravely walked out there, waving that white flag like crazy. A single shot ripped through him and his blue coat. *My* blue coat. He fell to his knees and then, on his face.

Our cannons boomed, knocking down some trees. A few of them came out of the woods. One was carrying a white flag of surrender. I wondered if the Captain would have us fire on them, but no, us Yankees had more humanity.

We took all of them prisoner and had them build a stockade for themselves.

The Estranged

I t's been said that most men lead lives of quiet desperation. For Carl Winters, this was an understatement. For the latter part of his sixty-six years, when he wasn't dwelling on the fact that he was alone, all alone, in his efficiency apartment, Carl engaged in his ritual of watching the TV news four times a day; morning, noon, evening and night. It distracted him from his own misery, knowing that there were others with much greater problems.

He only got dressed to go to the grocery store or, to the post office once or twice a week, after the news at noon. His errands took him about a mile from home and his 2002 Ford was still up to the task.

Carl always spent the time between newscasts to either nap, or lose himself in the reverie of the past; *his* past, back to a time when his life was less entangled with guilt and regret. *What's past, is past*, he told himself and concentrated on how he was going to handle the present, never mind the future. His Social Security check and government assistance took care of his rent and the few bills which were due on the same days every month. He liked the routine of sameness.

He had a daughter, Susan, who lived in Los Angeles with her husband, Bill and their two children, a boy, Nathan and a girl, Rosalie. Carl never met Bill, but understood that he had a good job so Susan didn't have to work. He also never met his grandchildren. He came to know the meaning of the word, "estrangement."

On the night stand, beside his bed, were two framed pictures of Nathan and Rosalie ... baby pictures. *Nathan has be ten by now and Rosalie, six. Maybe I should ask Susan to send me a couple of more recent pictures.* But, he knew that asking his daughter for anything was always difficult. Carl was never in his life very courageous, but that day had to be different. He hesitated for a moment, then looked up his daughter's phone number. She answered, sounding annoyed.

"The caller ID says it's you, Dad. What do you want *this* time?"

"I ... I just wanted to talk to you, Susie."

"You want money. Is that it?"

"I'd like to see my grandkids, before I get any older, that's all."

"Why? You've never seemed interested before. Never any birthday or Christmas presents, or even a card for either of them. You're a selfish, old man! That's what you are!"

"Okay, okay. That's what I am. Do you mind if I speak to them on the phone, at least?"

"Don't you know what time it is? They're both in school."

"Oh, I forgot about the time difference."

"You've forgotten about a lot of things, Dad. You forgot to come to my wedding, for one thing. Or, were you just too drunk! Our wedding pictures are all of me with *his* family!"

"Susie, I quit drinking a while back."

"Sure, like this morning?"

"I *did*, honest, and I want to make it up to you and your family. I really do and I want to come out for a little visit."

"How can you afford it? It has to cost, maybe, three-hundred dollars to fly out. Wait a minute, I'm not sending you the money, if that's what you're getting at. After Mom died, you started drinking pretty heavy, got fired from your job and blew everything you'd saved. You lost your house and walked away from a pension. You walked away from all of us."

Yeah, I taught seventh grade math. I couldn't teach those brats anything and the text book from which I had to teach, had the impossibly ludicrous title, Fun With Numbers. *Certainly, the publisher could've come up with a better title, than that!*

"Isn't Nathan having a birthday, soon? Maybe I can come out, then."

"Nathan had a birthday two months ago. Do you think you can get out here for Rosalie's birthday? It's next week."

"Next week? Do you think you can loan … ?"

"No, Dad, I'm not sending you any money. If you want to come out badly enough, you'll think of some way to do it. Every time I've sent you money, in the past, you just drank it away."

"But, I've told you … "

"Dad, that's final. Come out if you like or stay there. It makes no difference to us."

Susan hung up, leaving Carl with not very many choices. Reaching into the drawer of his nightstand, he pulled out his five-shot, .32

caliber revolver and as he held it, he seemed amused that it looked so small in his large hand. He pushed the little, fat bullets into the chambers. *One should be enough.* He put in five, anyway.

There was a bank next to the freeway. That would be the one. It had to happen. He planned to park in the lot next door and because there were surveillance cameras at the intersection leading to the freeway, he would drive back through town.

Carl walked in with a paper bag tucked under his arm and his .32 in his jacket pocket. He approached a young, female teller. "This window's closed," she told him and motioned toward the window on her right.

"You'll open this window for me," Carl whispered, "I have a gun, here's a bag. Fill it from your cash drawer. Don't say or do anything else, or I will shoot you. And keep your foot off the alarm button."

She did exactly as Carl had instructed. He placed the currency-filled bag inside his jacket, smiled, said, "thank you," and walked, nonchalantly out the door. He breathed hard all the way home, even for a while after he was home. He took out six-hundred dollars and put the rest of it in the closet. He didn't count what remained, but guessed that it was about five-thousand. Then, he lay on his bed and laughed. He couldn't actually believe that he'd done it. He laughed until he fell asleep.

When he awoke, he called in his flight reservation for the following morning. He would leave, bound for Los Angeles.

After the morning news, Carl was packed and waited for a cab. That day, he would be a generous tipper.

The walk through the security checkpoint went smoothly. They didn't suspect a thing. *But, why should they? So I've got three-hundred in my pocket and paid cash for my ticket, that's nothing to be suspicious about.*

He lumbered toward Gate 8, when he heard someone call his name, "Mr. Winters, wait a minute, sir." Carl turned to see a TSA agent and an airport police officer walking fast behind him.

Carl picked up his pace and soon began running, full-stride, with the men closing in. At six-five and one-hundred pounds overweight, the sudden exertion was too much for his heart. He pitched forward, cracking his skull on the floor.

Astonished, the police officer and the TSA agent slowed to a walk. The ticket agent at the gate came running over, shouting "Code Blue! Code Blue!" into her radio.

"What happened?" she asked, "he doesn't seem to be breathing. Do you suppose he's dead?"

The police officer answered, "I don't know, lady. It sure looks like it."

"Well," she said, "why were you guys chasing him?"

"I just wanted to give him his boarding pass," the TSA agent sighed, "The poor guy dropped it back there."

The Cheater

As most men want, so too Nick Harrison wanted more out of life. It would seem that he already had it all, but he wanted more. He didn't care if others called it a mid-life crisis. Maybe it was, after all. But, it didn't matter.

I am Peterson Motors' top salesman, the very best; not only on the lot, but probably in the entire city, even the state, he told his mirrored reflection.

Standing in the bathroom of his paid-for house, he tilted his head forward and scrutinized his dark, slightly receding, widow's peak. Satisfied, he showed himself a brilliantly white, capped-teeth smile. *Thanks, Mom for the hair gene.* A bit of graying, at the temples, only lent itself toward a distinguished appearance. Nick frowned each time he looked at his carefully trimmed, but gray mustache. Again, he had to use his wife's eyebrow pencil. *There, perfect.* He slid the knot of his tie, straightened it and off to meet another successful day. He had said countless times that the key to success was luck. All luck, nothing else. *Thanks Dad, for the lucky gene.*

This was only Nick's third dealership in twenty-three years; unusual in a cutthroat business where decent people don't possess proper survival skills.

It was a coin toss between Toyota and Nissan which determined Nick Harrison's decision to choose Nissan.

When Nick arrived at Nissan, the owner had unfortunately been doing his own TV commercials to save money. Being in front of a camera of any kind, was obviously not his strong suit, if he actually had one. Kenny Peterson was a short, balding, overweight man whose clothes were too tight. He also could barely read the cue cards. His biggest detriment, however, was that he spoke with a lisp, not slight, but heavy as *Sylvester* the cat's. Peterson did not achieve doing what he had hoped and that was to increase business. It may have dissuaded potential customers.

"Come in, Harrison," Peterson said, "what can I do for ya?"

"I've got an idea. I think it'll work. What if, and it wouldn't cost you anything. On the contrary, it'll make you money. A lot of it! I could take over doing the commercials.

Peterson realized that Nick was more photogenic, taller and hell, more handsome. And he's a good, no, a *great* salesman. Peterson clacked his laptop shut when Nick walked closer to the edge of his desk.

"You've got the job, but I can only increase your commission *if* you increase sales."

Peterson also doubled as sales manager, to save money.

It *did* increase business and as a bonus, it increased sales for Nick. In fact, he was becoming quite well-known. Nick Harrison had become the public face of Peterson Motors. As a consequence, he had to be careful regarding everything he did in public, everywhere he went. He was as recognizable as any local celebrity. He did have two sanctuaries where he could hide from prying eyes.

Nick had met the future Mrs. Harrison, an attractive, petite brunette, while they both attended the university; he, in his junior year and she, in pre-med. She wanted to be a doctor and he was undecided as to his career path, but would earn a B.A. in English, the following year.

Lynn and Nick moved in together in a small apartment within walking distance to the campus. Lynn soon saw the benefits to being engaged to a car salesman. Plus, he was making enough money to support both of them and he helped defray her tuition and textbook costs. They were well on their way to joining the masses of the middle-class and perhaps, beyond.

Lynn graduated from medical school in the top quarter of her class, applied for and received a fellowship of residency at the county hospital, downtown. A few years later, she had decided to specialize in cardiology and became as well-known in the medical community as Nick was as a TV pitchman and car salesman.

Being financially well-off, they bought a house in a gated community. But, twenty years later, as some marriages go, theirs was starting to erode. Lynn wanted at least one child and Nick preferred none. Lynn, in her forties, was worried that time was running out for her to conceive a child. Mr. Harrison, on the other hand, had an alternative mate, who kept him busy for the past couple of years.

Barbara, who was a year away from getting her degree in drama, lived in an apartment paid for, in cash, every month, by Nick Harrison. They had met when she bought a new Nissan from him. She needed a car to drive to school. A young redhead was a comfortable change for Nick and in exchange for paying her rent, she obliged by giving him free access to her apartment, as well as her body.

"**W**ho's Barbara Greene?" Lynn calmly asked.

"The name doesn't ring a bell. Why do you ask?"

Lynn's anger mounted. "Because you forgot to delete an email she sent you."

"You looked at my email? You spied?"

"Shut the hell up, Nick! How long has it been going on?"

"Honest to god, she means nothing to me!"

"Well, we'll see about that."

Unbeknownst to Nick, Lynn already had Barbara Greene's phone number. Had it memorized.

Barbara answered on the third ring.

"Hello, Barbara? This is Mrs. Harrison, Mrs. *Nick* Harrison. I'll get right to the point. I understand that you've been sleeping with my husband."

"Wha ... what? Who told you that?"

"I guessed, okay?"

"What do you want from me?"

"Since I'm in a position to control matters, I'm going to suggest a little game."

Nervously, Barbara asked, "A game? What kind of game?"

"We'll meet for coffee, or drinks on Tuesday next week, at the Ambassador Hotel. Be there and we'll discuss it. I'll be wearing a black dress."

Lynn arrived first and sat at the bar, keeping an eye on the doorway. Barbara walked in, a few minutes later and began looking around. Lynn slid off the barstool.

"Mrs. Harrison?"

"Yes. Let's sit in that booth. I'm drinking a martini. Care for one? I'm buying."

"Okay, that'd be nice." It took Barbara a few seconds to make eye contact. "What, may I ask, are you planning?"

"Oh, just a little surprise for Nick. Do you have anything I can use to scare him, like a large butcher knife?"

"Yes, but I also own a handgun, a Colt .38."

"Did *he* give it to you?"

"No, my dad did … taught me how to use it."

"This charade is going to work beautifully. He'll come to your apartment when he usually does, then you're going to put on the best acting performance of your life."

"Are you going to hurt him?"

"No," Lynn laughed, "no one gets hurt, but it'll scare the hell out of him. Let's meet at your apartment, in a couple of days."

oes Nick ring to be let in?

"He has keys."

"Isn't that just *precious?* Did you give him keys to your building and to your apartment, too?"

"Yes."

"Give me a long, sturdy screwdriver, if you've got one."

"I do. What're you going to do with it?"

"I'm going to pry the door away from the jamb, so it'll look like an unknown intruder broke in."

Lynn further explained that when Nick saw the damaged door, he would rush in and Barbara would lure him into the kitchen, with muffled sobs. Lynn would hold him at bay with the gun pressed against Barbara's right temple.

"Just be careful," Barbara warned, "There are live rounds in this gun." She pulled back the knob on the gun's left side, releasing the cylinder and showed it to Lynn. "See? All six bullets." Then, she gingerly clicked the cylinder back into place.

"Does it have a lot of recoil? A lot of kick?"

"Hardly any. I can shoot one-handed, but you might need to use two."

Lynn discovered, to her dismay, that Nick would come over twice, sometimes three times a week, whenever he told her that he was working late. When they stopped having sex, having a child became a moot point. Besides, she felt she was too old and a pregnancy would be dangerous.

Nick had told Barbara that Lynn could never have any kids. A lie told convincingly. He could see that she was older, her figure turned matronly, making her, in his mind, less sexually attractive. Barbara, on the other hand, was more appealing; more beautiful than cute, taller and slimmer.

"Okay, when Nick comes running, trying to save you, you've got to use that acting talent. Pretend you're scared out of your wits, in fear for your life. This might even earn yourself a *Cleo* or, *Tony*, whatever they call it."

"I really don't need direction, Lynn." She looked at her watch. "He should be here in about ten minutes."

"Places everyone!" Lynn said, cheerfully and slipped on a pair of surgical gloves.

When he saw the broken door, Nick Harrison didn't have to surmise that anything was amiss, as he barreled into the kitchen and halted abruptly when he saw his wife holding a pistol to his girlfriend's head. Lynn's left hand was a doubled fist under Barbara's chin. Nick noticed that Barbara, the taller of the two, had her knees bent. Her hair was matted to her forehead with sweat and in her eyes, was a look of sheer terror. Because of the pressure on her jaw, she had to speak through her teeth. "Please help me," she pleaded.

"Get over there, Nick!" Lynn growled, motioning with her head. "All right, the name of the game is about choices. Who're you going to choose?"

Nick wisely knew that when it came to choices, always choose the woman with the gun. But, in this instance, his reply came too slowly.

Lynn took the gun away from Barbara's temple and fired. Nick reeled back two steps; felt inside his black sport coat, to his shoulder, withdrew his hand and looking at his fingers, shouted, "You shot me! My god, you shot me!"

"I told you to choose! You choose!" She squeezed the trigger once more, aiming at his chest.

Nick looked at his wife in disbelief. "Why, why baby? Oh, shit!" and dropped to his knees. As he pitched forward, he put his hands out to break his fall.

Lynn let loose her grip on Barbara.

"You killed him! You said you were only going to *scare* him!"

"So what? He got what he deserved. Here's your gun, sweetheart. I guess you won't get to have him, either. A neighbor of yours probably called the police and they'll be on the way. I'll be leaving now."

Lynn, on her way out the door, looked back at Nick lying on his face. She took another look, when she saw Nick rise to one knee. She also saw Barbara with the gun in both hands, arms extended. Now, it was Lynn who was terrified. Barbara cocked the hammer back with her left thumb, so it wouldn't change her aim and fired, catching Lynn in the stomach, causing her to double over. Then, another shot to her head. Lynn collapsed near the door. Dead, before she hit the floor.

Both of them were momentarily deafened and had to shout. "It's a good thing I told you to wear that black jacket, so she wouldn't see any blood.

"I loaded three blanks in the first three chambers, just to be sure. The other three were live and when I fired single-action, the cylinder skipped over the blank and moved to the next chamber."

Nick chuckled, "I didn't even know that. Anyway, hon, you shot an *intruder*. I'm so proud of you!"

"The police'll want to take my gun. I've got one round left. Nick, why don't you stand over there, by your wife's body?"

"Why?"

Lynn pointed the gun at him. "Just do it!"

Nick did as he was told and asked again, "Why? What're you gonna do?"

A bullet hit him in the heart. He spun and fell near his wife.

Lynn heard several police officers rumbling up the stairs. She opened the gun's cylinder and placed the weapon on the floor.

Two policemen came rushing through the door. "What happened here?"

"What the hell does it look like? These assholes tried to break in."

The Legend - A five-act play

Characters in order of appearance:

1. Joey Donnetelli
2. bartender / bouncer
3. Frank Kaminski, talent agent
4. Maria, Joey's wife
5. Rusty, Mr. Weiss' bodyguard
6. Mr. Weiss
7. Nick Kaminski, Frank's dad
8. Al Jolson
9. Benny Goodman
10. Man #1, also #1
11. Man #2, also #2
12. Detective #3
13. Voice of airline captain
14. Hotel bellhop

Act I, Scene 1

The scene opens at the **Black Cat,** *a small nightclub in New York City. The year is 1943. Joey Donnetelli is a band singer who doesn't quite realize his true potential as a possible rising star. Things change when Joey meets Frank Kaminski.*

Donnetelli is a nice-looking man, in his late twenties with dark, wavy hair. He is dressed in a dark double-breasted suit, white shirt and dark tie.

Smattering of light applause is heard as amber stage lights come up. A liquor bar is positioned upstage right so that the back of the bar is seen.

Joey enters stage right, loosens his tie, opens his jacket, sits at the bar and lights a cigarette. Wide amber spot on Joey.

The bartender steps in from stage right with an ashtray and a drink. The dark, amber drink is about four-fingers-deep, in a stout glass.

Bartender: *[Flatly.]* Good set, Joey.

Joey: *[Wearily.]* Yeah, thanks.

Frank Kaminski enters from stage right. He is dressed casually in a patterned brown sweater. Kaminski's younger than Joey ... in his early twenties. He walks behind Joey and sits on Joey's right. Joey, at first ignores him and stares down at his drink.

Kaminski: *[Sincerely.]* Mr. Donnetelli, I just wanna say that I really like your work. That song, especially that song, "Let's Give It A Try." It's just perfect the way you do it. Why, it could be your theme song!

Joey: *[Slightly aggravated.]* So, what's your con, kid? Or, maybe yer some kinda fruit, or somethin'.

Kaminski: *[Defensively.]* Hey, I'm not a fruit! I got a wife and a coupla kids!

Joey: *[Increasingly aggravated.]* Everybody's got a wife and a coupla kids. Now, what the hell's your con?

Kaminski: *[Takes a business card from his pocket and slides it in front of Joey.]* I'm an agent, Mr. Donnetelli. You need an agent?

Joey: *[Finally looks at Kaminski.]* No, I don't need any agent ... *[Pauses, looks at card.]* I got a good gig, right here ... free drinks [takes a gulp of his drink], free food [takes another gulp, finishes it and points to the glass. *[The bartender re-enters, takes the empty glass and returns with another drink.]* I'm one week into an eight-week contract, two shows a night, a decent house band and it pays the rent. Okay? So, get the hell away from me!

Kaminski: *[Pleading.]* But, Mr. Donnetelli, you're so much better than this. Just look around at this dive. Whadda ya see? A bunch of mobsters and their wives or, girlfriends or, hookers. You got more class! They don't appreciate good singin' or, good performin'. I been sittin' in the back for two nights and I can tell ya, that you're different. You got a different kinda sound. Real smooth-like!

Joey: *[Sarcastically.]* So, book me inta the Garden. I'm sure the Knicks won't mind movin' over for me. You book me in there, kid, and you got yourself a deal!

Kaminski: *[Pleading again.]* But, Mr. Donnetelli ...

Joey: *[Resolutely.]* The answer's no! Now, get outta here! Can't ya see I'm on break? *[Joey motions for the bartender. The bartender re-enters as Kaminski exits, stage right. Joey leans forward to the bartender.]*

Joey: [*Loud whisper.*] Listen, that guy's one of those stage-door-johnnies. When I'm done tonight, I want somebody to go out in the alley and see if he's hangin' around.

Bartender: Yeah, Joey, I'll do it. If he's out there, do ya want me to take care of 'im?

Joey: No. No rough stuff, understand? Just make him go away. I don't want to run into him outside. Okay?

Bartender: Whatever you say, Joey. He won't be there. Who is he, by the way?

Joey: Just some jerky punk, tryin' to get in on the action.

Fade to black.

I, Scene 2

Iin the alley. The stage is dimly lit, except for an overhead spot or, light above the stage door. Joey enters, upstage left. Freezes in his tracks and stares. The bartender lays at his feet, moaning.

Kaminski: [*From the darkness.*] Mr. Donnetelli, over here. It's me.

Joey: [*Peering out, surprised.*] What the hell? What happened? What'd you do to 'im?

Kaminski: [*Almost apologetically.*] He charged at me and I gave 'im a right cross. That's all.

Then, he just kinda sagged. Should we help 'im up and see if he's all right?

Joey: Nah, screw 'im. Let the stupe lay there! [*Joey steps over the bartender.*] You been comin' here for a coupla nights to see me?

Kaminski: Yeah, this'll be the third night.

Joey: Maybe I could use a tough guy like you.

Kaminski: Oh, I'm not so tough. He was just too slow.

Joey: [*Pulls out Kaminski's card and squints at it.*] Kaminski, huh? Is that Russian or, Polish?

Kaminski: It's Polish. Why?

Joey: I don't know. Just askin'. The card says that you're union. What other clients ya got? [the two walk slowly down stage right.]

Kaminski: Mostly variety acts. You name it. But, no crooners. At least, not yet.

Joey: So, you think I got what it takes, huh?

Kaminski: Yeah, I really think so.

Joey: Well, okay then, kid. It's a deal! You get me some decent gigs, away from padded sewers like this and I'll pay you ten percent. I'll give ya my phone number.

Kaminski: Okay, I can even start tomorrow. How'd that be?

Joey: Great! By the way, Kaminski, why ain't you over fightin' the War?

Kaminski: 4-F.

Joey: Me, too. At least we got that in common. *[They both look back at the bartender who's starting to get up. He's brushing himself off and sees Joey and Kaminski.]*

Joey: *[To Kaminski.]* C'mon, let's get outta here!

Lights fade to black, curtain falls.

Act II
Scene 1

Lights come up as curtain rises. Joey Donnetelli's wife, Maria, is introduced in this scene.

The scene begins in Joey's kitchen, at mid-morning, on a weekday. His apartment is small and Spartan. Joey is dressed in a white t-shirt. His suspenders hang down over gray pants. He takes a sip of coffee, then sets the cup down on a small, wooden table which is positioned under the kitchen window. He sighs, places his hands on the table, leans forward and looks upward out the window. The neighboring building casts a shadow over his apartment building.

Joey: *[To himself.]* We had to get a place where we never get to see the goddam sun!

Maria: *[From off-stage.]* What?

Joey: *[Toward Maria's voice.]* Just talkin' to myself. *[Louder.]* We need to move somewheres else. I mean, this is a helluva place to raise any kids!

Maria: *[Still off-stage]*. Not yet, Joey. We talked about that.

Maria enters from downstage, right. Joey straightens up, takes a step back and watches her enter. Maria is wearing a beige, summer dress with puffed sleeves, at the shoulders. Her long, dark hair is pinned up and she is wearing deep, red lipstick on her full lips. She reaches for Joey's coffee and takes a sip, wipes off the rim with her thumb, then stands between Joey and the table. Maria is slim and with her hair done in that manner, is noticeably taller than Joey. She leans on the table, facing Joey.

Maria: We need a new mirror in the bathroom. It's got a crack in it. I heard it's gonna be hot today. That's why I'm wearin' this. How do I look? *[Turns one leg toward Joey.]* Are my seams straight? Have ya heard from that guy? That agent of yours? I hope ya didn't give him any money up front.

Joey: It's only been a coupla days. He'll call me if he's got anything. And no, I didn't give him any money. This is how it works, Maria. He don't get paid unless I get paid.

Maria: Joey, I don't know about the business you're in. Poppa says that you got your head in the clouds. I didn't dare tell him that you quit your job on the docks. He thinks you're still workin' there and the singin' thing is just a hobby.

Joey: [Defensively.] First of all, your Poppa needs to keep his opinions to himself. And as far as money is concerned, I can make more money singin' for a few hours than I can make all week, slavin' down at the docks. Maybe I can make enough money so we can move outta this joint. This place! This place is another one of your Poppa's and your Mama's ideas. They want you close by! They got off the boat from the old country and pitched their tent right here. They're never gonna move! But, we are and for once, they're not gonna stop us.

Maria: Is this agent gonna get ya a better engagement somewheres else? Outta that awful dive?

Joey: Yeah, he says that he will.

Maria: *[Looks at her watch.]* Are you goin' out today?

Joey: I don't know. Maybe. Kaminski's 'sposed to call me today, so I guess I better hang around for awhile.

Maria: Well, I gotta go to work, now. Good luck. I hope somethin' happens, soon. *[Joey leans in to kiss her.]* Just a peck, Joey. Lipstick. *[Joey smiles and gives her a peck. Maria exits, stage right.]*

Joey watches her leave, then turns to look out the window, again. He takes another sip of his coffee. A look of disgust crosses his face, as he places the cup down hard. He lights a cigarette and rubs the back of his neck. The phone rings twice. Joey answers.

Joey: Kaminski! Where the hell are ya? It sounds like you're in a rain barrel, or somethin'. *[Joey takes the phone over by the window and looks out and down toward the street.]* Are ya comin' up? Okay, okay. Quit talkin'. Just come up. *[Joey goes to the counter top where he finds a quart bottle of whiskey and pours himself a drink, about three-fingers deep. Still looking out the window, takes a small sip. It's only moments, when there's a flurry of rapid knocks at the door. Joey, at first, is startled.]*

Kaminski: *[Off-stage.]* Joey! It's me! Open up!

Joey: [surprised] Already? Wha'd ya do, run all the way? [Joey crosses to stage right, carrying the drink with him. Opens door. Kaminski, out of breath, stumbles in, carrying an old suitcase and has a newspaper folded under his arm.]

Kaminski: *[Gulping for air.]* You won't believe this, Joey, you just won't believe this!

Joey: *[Laughing.]* I probly won't.

Kaminski: *[Looks at Joey's glass, astonished.]* You're drinkin' before noon, even? Go easy on that stuff, willya? It's bad for your pipes. Those cigarettes, too.

Joey: *[Notices suitcase, points.]* Goin' on a trip, Kaminski?

Kaminski: No. I'll tell ya about it in a coupla minutes. Have ya seen today's paper? *[Hands Joey the paper.]* Feast your eyes, Joey. Page four. I got a critic to go over and review your show, last night.

Joey: *[Glances at Kaminski, while he turns the pages.]* I don't see it. Wait. Here it is.

Kaminski: *[Anxiously.]* Read it, Joey. Read it out loud!

Joey: *[Crosses back to kitchen table and spreads out newspaper.]* Let's see. It says: "I went to a small, seedy club called, 'The Black Cat,' last night and was mildly surprised at the quality of the entertainment. While the band was only average, the boy singer seemed out of his element. By that, I mean he was far superior in comparison to the venue. His phrasing and song presentation were superb! Instead of following the song and the band, he had a tendency to lead it. The women in attendance appeared to enjoy his shy smile and nonchalant style of crooning. I could hear them sigh every time he looked at them, much to the surprise of their male companions. It is my considered opinion that this young man will give Bing Crosby a run for his money. Go and see him. You needn't get too dressed up." *[Angry, throws the paper* *on the floor.]* The creep didn't say my name! He mentions Crosby! He didn't even say my name, Kaminski!

Kaminski: Take it easy, Joey. It's still recognition. They'll flock to see ya. People will be curious to see the new, mystery singer! And thousands of people read his column every day!

Joey: *[Peevishly.]* But, he could've at least said my name.

Kaminski: It's a start. This is only the beginnin', Joey. Maybe Winchell'll write the next review!

Joey: Yeah, and maybe I'll be tellin' Maria that we're movin' to Park Avenue. By the way, Kaminski, [laughs] I think I liked you better when I was Mister Donnetelli.

Kaminski: *[Cryptically.]* Well, you could be movin', we both could be movin' to Park Avenue, sooner than ya think.

Joey: What're you talkin' about?

Kaminski: I mean, we're on our way, Joey. The big time! Stick with me and we'll be rich as Sultans!

Joey: When is this gonna happen?

Kaminski: I been workin' on it. [proudly] I got you a two-week engagement at the Club Rio with an extension option. Five hundred smackers a week, Joey! Just think! And you don't hafta be afraid to bring Maria, 'cause the Mob don't own it!

Joey: *[Very interested.]* The Club Rio? That's kind of a swank place, ain't it? [angry] Wait a minute. Hold it. I got four weeks left at the Black Cat. They're not gonna let me outta the contract. These guys, they don't screw around! I could wind up as an anchor on a tuna boat!

Kaminski: Joey, listen. They'll let you finish your contract. These people at the Club Rio understand your situation.

Joey: *[Calming down, pulls out a chair and motions for Kaminski to sit down.]* Want some coffee? I'll heat it up.

Kaminski: No thanks. You better save that paper for your wife. Maybe she'll cut out the review and save it in a scrapbook. Hey, now I got some more news for ya. We don't get paid nothin', but it's exposure. The Black Cat'll let you do this, for sure. They're pretty patriotic.

Joey: *[Impatiently.]* What. I'm all ears.

Kaminski: There's gonna be a War Bond Rally at Roseland and you are gonna be in it. All the big names are gonna do it. It's gonna be this Saturday night. The newsreels'll be there. It's gonna be on the radio. They'll probly record the thing, too.

Joey: *[Pensively.]* Yeah, they should let me out of the contract for only one night.

Kaminski: And it'll prove to some of the saps out there that you're just as patriotic as anybody else. That you're anti-Fascist. You know what I mean?

Joey: 'Cause I'm Italian, right? Big names are gonna be there? Like who?

Kaminski: They're callin' it, "A Night of a Thousand Stars." They've got twenty performers lined up.

Joey: A thousand? And they only have twenty? Where do they get a thousand?

Kaminski: It sounds better than "A Night of Twenty Stars," don't it? Anyway, Broadway stars'll be there. The Barrymores' will be there. Everybody who's somebody …

Joey: What're they gonna do, read Shakespeare?

Kaminski: No, they're gonna be in the audience. They'll be introduced. They'll stand up and take bows. And that'll be worth about a grand in pledges. Now, here's how the line-up goes: Each singer gets to do three songs and each dancer, one dance number. They booked Kelly and Astaire! They'll start with the newer talent and then, the older ones.

Joey: Where do I fit in?

Kaminski: Right after Sinatra.

Joey: So, who gets to close the show.

Kaminski: Jolson. Jolson always closes.

Joey: *[Laughs.]* How many songs does he get to do? As if I didn't know.

Kaminski: *[Also laughs.]* About eight, with five encores. They pretty much let him do what he wants, 'cause he raises a lot, I mean a lot of money.

Joey: Who're the bands and what songs do I do?

Kaminski: They got Goodman and Dorsey. I think I'm gonna have ya do *Pennies From Heaven*, upbeat, and a little bit slower tempo with, *Anything Goes* and saving the best for last, your theme song, *Let's Give It A Try*. I'm tellin' ya, it's gonna be fantastic! Everybody's gonna rehearse in the afternoon. Another thing, Joey, ditch the double-breasted. It makes ya look too short. Get a black, or navy two-button, okay? And ya might wanna add a quarter-inch to your heels.

Joey: I guess if I wanna play ball with the big boys, I gotta let you call the shots.

Kaminski: [ignoring Joey's comment] Yeah, I think they did this show six months ago, or somethin' and they raised fifty grand! Crosby and Sinatra were credited for raising at least half of it! By the way, Sinatra always draws a buncha bobby-soxers. So, they'll be screamin' for him and the best part is, they'll probly stay and scream for you, too.

Joey: So, I get Frankie's leftovers, huh? Besides, how do I know that they'll be screamin' for me?

Kaminski: Oh, they will. Trust me.

Joey: *[Focuses attention to Kaminski's suitcase.]* You haven't told me what's in the suitcase, yet.

Kaminski: Oh, here. Lemme show ya. [crosses, gets suitcase, re-crosses and sits down. Opens suitcase.] Neckties. I bought out a vendor's entire stock and suitcase.

Joey: They're kinda loud, ain't they? *[Shakes head.]* Oh, no. You're not thinkin' of havin' me wear 'em …

Kaminski: *[Forcefully.]* Yeah. It's your new trademark! Here's what I want ya to do. You can start doin' it on Saturday. Remember, trust me. I know of what I speak. Don't worry, these are real cheap ties, cheap material. While the band intros your theme song, you loosen your tie. You get to the last stanza and you untie it and let it hang there. Then, at the end of it, you throw it to the girls in the crowd. They'll scream! They'll go crazy! They'll fight over it!

Joey: Why the hell do I need a gimmick like that?

Kaminski: 'Cause everybody else's got one. Sinatra does that thing with his mouth. *[Moves his lower lip to the side, exaggerating the gesture and moving his head at the same time.]* The girls scream, so he keeps doin' it. It's a gimmick. Crosby buh, buh, bubba boos, the girls swoon. Jolson gets down on one knee, spreads his arms and the crowd goes nuts! Well, ya know what? I gotta get goin'. I gotta a lotta work to do before Saturday. *[Gets up and begins crossing toward door.]* So, I'll see ya Saturday at two, sharp! Just come in the stage door.

Joey: Yeah, but are ya sure ya know what you're doin'? Do ya think we can really pull this off?

Kaminski: Relax, Joey. You're in good hands. *[Exits]*

Joey watches Kaminski exit, then turns away.

Stage lights fade to black.

II, Scene 2

Joey comes to work at the Black Cat for an evening performance. It is a Friday night ... the night before Joey's scheduled appearance at the War Bond rally.

Introduced in this scene, are the owner and manager of the Black Cat, Mr. Weiss and his assistant, Rusty. Rusty is a large, red-haired, young man. Mr. Weiss is a small, slender, middle-aged man with dark, slicked-back hair, parted in the middle. A dim, overhead spot shines on Joey as he enters, center stage right. The sound of people talking and the tinkle of glasses is faintly heard. The formidable figure of Rusty appears from the shadows and stands in front of Joey.

Joey: *[Startled]* Hiya, Rusty. *[Takes a step back.]*

Rusty: Mr. Weiss wants to see ya.

Joey: I'm on stage in five minutes. *[Tries to walk past Rusty.]*

Rusty: *[Moves in front of Joey.]* Now, Joey. Mr. Weiss wants to see you now. *[Extends his arm to point the way.]*

Background noise fades, as amber overhead spot comes on and reveals a desk, set at a forty-five-degree angle. Other spot dims and goes out. Mr. Weiss is seated behind the desk and turns on a banker's lamp with a green shade. His elbows rest on the desk, his fingers are steepled and pressed against his lips. Rusty circles behind Weiss and stands with his hands clasped.

Weiss: *[Smiling.]* Come in, Joey. Sit down. *[Gestures toward a chair in front of the desk. Joey pulls the chair out a few inches, sits and leans forward attentively.]* I'm very disturbed at what I've been hearing. Frankly, I'm disappointed in you, Joey.

Joey: What's this all about, Mr. Weiss?

Weiss: First of all, shut your mouth. Second of all ... it's that Kaminski character. That weasel and his old man run the biggest con in town.

Joey: I, I don't understand.

Weiss: [*Puts a finger to his lips.*] Shhh, shhh. I don't like some, little, two-bit punk, son of a bitch, KOing my best bartender. Kaminski did that and he's never coming near this place, again. Don't you know what he's up to? [*Joey shakes his head.*] He goes around to all the small clubs and tells singers, comics, jugglers and whoever, how great they are. Then, he has them join the union and books them into the Club Rio. Do you wanna know who owns the Club Rio? I'll tell you who. Nick Kaminski. Sound familiar? That's your Frank Kaminski's old man. Oh, sure, the Club Rio's a nice place. During Prohibition, Joey, it was a Speak. Liquor downstairs and a whorehouse upstairs. [*Sarcastically.*] Real respectable, those Kaminski's, but real smart, too! Now, all of a sudden, they're legitimate or, so it would seem.

Joey: So, what kinda con do ya think they're pullin'?

Weiss: I thought I told you to shut-up and listen. You're just another victim. As I said, they tell you that you're great and sign you to a contract. Short-term. Usually just a week or, two. Then, they tell you that you need a manager and raise the split to twenty percent. Yes, half a grand a week is a lot of money for somebody starting out, but after a week or so, they fire you and drop you like a hot potato. Presto, [rubs his hands together and opens his arms] you're out of work and nobody else hires you because you're not that good! What's your little wife, Maria isn't it? What's she gonna say about that? Say, let me tell ya about a ventriloquist they hired and fired. He got depressed and committed suicide … shot his dummy first, then shot himself. The newspapers got ahold of it and called it a murder-suicide. [*Laughs.*]

Joey: Well, don't you think I'm a good singer, Mr. Weiss?

Weiss: You're average, kid. You're average. But, I brought you here because I thought you had a little talent. Good enough for this place. Kaminski's pushing you too fast. Leading you down the wrong path. You're not ready for the big time. Hell, you're not even ready for the Club Rio.

Joey: What exactly do ya want me to do?

Weiss: I want you to go ahead and do the Bond Rally tomorrow night. When you're done singing, come over here. You're still under contract. By the way, your little friend, Kaminski, won't be there.

Joey: Why not?

Weiss: [*Turns and smiles at Rusty.*] Because he had an accident.

Joey: [*Shocked.*] What? What happened?

Weiss: He fell down. Right, Rusty? *[Rusty nods.]* Broke his leg in two places. But, he'll be all right, except that his new nickname'll be "step-and-a-half." *[Chuckles.]* Rusty, how long has Joey got to go on his contract?

Rusty: Four weeks.

Weiss: What a coincidence! That's about when Kaminski gets out of the hospital. Now, about your contract, Joey. *[Slides paper across desk]*. I want to call your attention to the last page, just above where you signed it. *[Joey leans in and looks carefully.]* Read it. I want to hear what it says. It says that I'm the "party of the first part" and you're the "party of the second part."

Joey: *[Looks at Weiss, then at the papers and begins.]* "Party of the first part may cancel this contract at any time, party of the first part desires. Furthermore, party of the first part, at party of the first part's sole discretion, may extend the contract to any length, whatsoever."

Weiss: Good. There, you see? And you signed it. Is there any place where it says, "party of the second part?"

Joey: No, it don't. Are you gonna extend the contract past four weeks?

Weiss: No, I'm throwing you to the Kaminski's. You can learn your lesson the hard way. Rusty, tell Joey what happened to that newspaper columnist … the one who wrote that ridiculous review … calling this place, my place, "seedy."

Rusty: No, you go ahead. You tell it much better.

Weiss: He's unemployed, so to speak. And if you, [points at Joey] or anybody else thinks that newspaper people can come in here anytime they feel like it and write whatever they want, well … And I think that because of that review, there might be screaming teenage girls trying to get in here to see you … I'm telling you that it's not going to happen. Listen, Joey, my clientele are businessmen who come here, with their wives, to drink a little and dance a little and listen to [raises voice] background music. That's you, Joey. You're nothing but background. That's all, Joey. You can go to work now and remember to mind your manners if you don't want to wind up as Kaminski's roommate.

Joey gets up. The band is heard, softly, then volume increases, playing "Stardust" in 4/4 time. Lights fade slowly to black. Curtain falls.

Act III, Scene 1

A white spot comes up and shines on Joey Donnetelli who's standing in the wings of the stage at Roseland Ballroom. An older man is standing next to him. Nick Kaminski is introduced in this scene.

Nick: *[Enthusiastically.]* You look great, Joey! Silk suit and everything! Look, kid, don't be nervous. I know this is your big shot at this. I handed your arrangement to the band, so you're all set. You go on after Sinatra.

Joey: Who the hell are you?

Nick: I'm Nick Kaminski, Frank's dad. He's in the hospital, ya know. I'm fillin' in for him.

Joey: And you guys own the Club Rio?

Nick: Correction. I own the Club. He just works for me.

Joey: Why didn't you show up at rehearsal, this afternoon?

Nick: 'Cause I was visitin' my boy in the hospital. He'll be listenin' to the whole thing on the radio. Say, do ya know who else'll be listenin'? Right here in the audience? I already saw some of 'em ... big wigs from the union, RCA and Columbia Records ... other club owners, Broadway stars ... everybody! Don't be nervous, though. Pretend that it's just another gig at the Black Rat.

Joey: You mean the Black Cat?

Nick: Sure, kid. That's what I meant.

Nick sees another man coming his way and steps aside. Joey doesn't see him. The man is short, balding and has a deep tan.

Man: *[As he brushes past Joey, speaking quickly.]* Pardon me, sonny.

Joey: Was that who I think it was?

Nick: *[Nonchalantly.]* Yeah, that was Jolson. He's probly gonna tell the band that he wants all his songs played in E-flat. By the way, you'll be singin' with Goodman.

Screams, cheers and loud applause are heard, drowning out the bands last few notes. Quick fade to blackout.

Nick: *[Looks toward stage.]* Get ready kid. Get out there before they stop clappin'. I almost forgot; you're gonna do "Let's Give It A Try" first, instead of last. And don't forget to move the microphone stand over, just a little bit. *[Nick pats Joey on the back.]* Go! Get out there! Sing to those bobbysoxers!

Joey looks back at Nick as the overhead spot fades and stage lights come up, revealing the bandleader, Benny Goodman. Goodman is holding a clarinet, has dark, slicked-back hair, parted high on the left side. He is wearing round, black-framed glasses. Goodman is shown leading a band which is offstage and unseen. Band begins playing "Let's Give It A Try." Joey approaches mic stand, at center stage and moves it a foot closer to the band. Girls begin screaming, a little. Goodman, surprised, mouths the words, "What the hell?"

Joey: *[Begins singing. Loosens his necktie.]* "If you're so inclined, my love, and if the stars above, say it's right for us, then let's give it a try." *[Screams grow louder.]* "Let our hearts soar into love. Let's give it a try, just you and I. Under the stars above, I'll pledge you my love." *[Joey unites his tie. More screams.]* "So, if you're inclined, my love, and if the stars above, say it's right for us, let our hearts soar into love. Let's give it a try, just you and I ... just you and I."

Joey takes off his tie, rolls it into a ball and throws it into the screaming crowd. The screams are deafening as stage lights fade. The last bar of "Anything Goes" is faintly heard. Overhead spot comes on, in the wings, stage right. Two large men, wearing hats wait for Joey to enter wings.

Man #1: *[Throws white towel toward Joey.]* Here, you might need this. *[Joey catches towel and mops sweat from his face and neck.]*

Joey: Thanks. You guys seen a short, fat guy? He was right here a few minutes ago.

Man #2: You mean Kaminski? He's on his way downtown.

Joey: Yeah? Well, who are you?

Man #2: Police. We'd like ya to come with us. You know, to answer a few questions.

Joey: A few questions? About what? What's this all about?

Man #1: We'll tell ya when we get downtown. 'Cmon, we'll give ya a ride. *[Turns and says to Man #2.]* God, I hate dealin' with these small-time hoods!

The three men exit as lights fade.

III, Scene 2

The stage is bare, except for three folding chairs at center stage. Joey Donnetelli is seated, facing stage left. A tight, white overhead spot shines on him. The other two folding chairs are, one to his right and one two feet directly in front of him. The two large men, from the previous scene are standing. They are now called Detective #1 and #2.

Detective #2 takes off his coat and hangs it on the back of the chair to Joey's right and stands with his hands on his hips, alternately folding his arms. Detective #1 turns a chair around and sits in front of Joey. He holds a clipboard, glances at it and at Joey. He leans forward and begins talking.

Det. #1: Do ya know what this is? *[Holds up clipboard.]*

Joey: *[Nervously.]* No, what?

Det. #1: It's your confession. All typed up, nice and neat.

Joey: *[Baffled, looks at detectives.]* Confession? What for?

Det. #2: *[Circling behind Joey.]* I think we'll start with a real simple question. Where did you go after you got done workin' at the Black Cat, last night?

Joey: *[Craning his neck to see Det. #2.]* I got done at One and went home.

Det. #1: Are you sure? I mean, sometimes you guys stay and drink, or play cards, or somethin'.

Joey: *[Defiantly.]* I was in bed by 2:30. You can ask my wife.

Det. #2: *[Positions himself to Joey's right, with hands on hips.]* Maybe we'll just do that.

Joey: I'll ask ya, again. What's this all about?

Det. #2: *[Mockingly.]* What's this all about? That's what you all say. Ya know Al Weiss? The owner of the Black Cat?

Joey: Yeah, I work for him. In fact, I got about fifteen minutes to get over there.

Det. #1: Well, you're not gonna be workin' there for a few days. Neither is anybody else.

Joey: Why, what happened?

Det. #1: Okay, we'll tell ya. Somebody threw a coupla gasoline bombs at his front doors, last night. Nobody was hurt, but the place is gonna be closed for a few days. We think it was Nick Kaminski and somebody else. We have reason to believe that maybe you're that somebody else. We're sweatin' ol' man Kaminski in the next room, right now. It's a good thing we grabbed him at Roseland, before Weiss got ahold of him.

Joey: I just told you, I went home! I don't know anything else that happened in the middle of the night.

Det. #2: Look, Joey, we're tryin' to nip this little war between Weiss and Kaminski, in the bud, before it gets outta hand, understand? First, Weiss had Kaminski's kid beat up … they almost killed him and now, this. It's like a puzzle and you're one of the pieces. You small-timers … ya give the big-time hoods a bad name!

Just then, another detective with sleeves rolled-up, loosens tie and mopping forehead with handkerchief, enters, stage left, laughing. Spotlight widens.

Det. #3: You can let this guy go. I got a full confession outta ol' man Kaminski!

Det. #1: *[Stands and slams clipboard on the chair.]* Aw, shit!

Det. #3: *[Jubilantly.]* Yeah, I think the D.A. himself, is gonna prosecute! Kaminski and his little playmates'll get at least ten years!

Joey: *[Stands and says to the three detectives.]* If you'll excuse me, gentlemen, I'll be leavin' now. *[Brashly.]* Thanks for your, uh, hospitality.

Det. #1: Just a minute, you. We're not done with you, yet. Sit back down. *[Joey sits.]* I just don't understand why a guy like you, a guy with your talent, wants to get mixed-up with people like Weiss and Kaminski and wants to have screamin' teenage girls runnin' after him. Answer me, that.

Joey: *[Shrugs.]* Now that I think about it, I sure as hell don't know. And, as far as the screamin' girls … I guess that comes with the territory.

Det. #1: Well, take my advice and get away from those people.

Joey: Okay, can I go now?

Det. #1: Yeah. [swings his arm towards door] Get outta here!

Joey exits as the three men follow him and exit.

Act IV, Scene 1

Two years have passed. It is now 1945. The scene is in Joey Donnetelli's kitchen, appearing the same as in Act II, Scene 1. Lights come up as curtain rises. Joey's wife, Maria is sitting at the kitchen table, by the window, drinking coffee. It is mid-morning.

There's a series of rapid knocks at the door. Maria is startled out of her reverie and crosses to answer the door. Frank Kaminski appears.

Kaminski: *[Excitedly.]* Hi, Maria! Is Joey home?

Maria: Just a minute. Joey, *[Calls off-stage.]* Frank Kaminski's here.

Joey: *[Answers from off-stage.]* Kaminski? Well, tell him to get-out-ski!

Maria: He'll be right out. *[Calls again.]* Joey!

Joey enters, fastening his bathrobe.

Joey: What the hell do you want, Kaminski? Dontcha know it's Sunday?

Kaminski: Yeah, yeah. I just wanted to tell ya that you're the "Toast of the Town!"

Joey: What's that s'posed to mean?

Kaminski: It's right here in the Daily News. Sullivan's column! He mentions ya twice! *[Hands Joey the newspaper.]* Page fourteen! Maria, you should cut that out for your scrapbook!

Joey: Ed Sullivan was there, last night? I didn't see 'im.

Kaminski: Joey, he sends other people when he's busy.

Joey: *[Finds page fourteen.]* Here it is. God, he even spelled my name right!

Kaminski: See, Joey, you're on your way!

Joey: On my way to what? You been sayin' that for a coupla years, now.

Kaminski: Hey, I didn't come over here just to show ya the newspaper. Guess who got ya a recordin' session with Columbia?

Joey: What?

Maria: *[Excitedly.]* Joey! A recordin' session! Think of it!

Kaminski: Your A-side'll be, *Let's Give it a Try* and the B-side'll be, *Stardust*.

Joey: Everybody's done *Stardust*. Besides, I can't sing it with that standard arrangement.

Kaminski: Don't worry, they'll tailor the arrangement to fit ya.

Joey: Okay, so when do we go over there?

Kaminski: Not over there, Joey, out there. We're gonna be flyin' to L.A.!

Maria: How long, Joey? How long will ya be out there? [Joey shrugs. Maria glowers at Kaminski] How long, Frank?

Kaminski: About four days. Now, here's the best part of all: I set up a screen test at Fox!

Maria: The movies, Frank? The movies? Joey, why didn't ya tell me?

Joey: 'Cause I don't know what the hell he's talkin' about. This is the first time I heard about it. Only four days? Are ya sure, Kaminski?

Kaminski: Yeah, four days. But, there's a lotta work to be done, before we go. I know a woman who can give both of us diction and elocution lessons, so when we get to L.A., we don't sound like a coupla yokels who just fell off a turnip truck.

Joey: Speak for yourself!

Maria: Joey don't need no diction or electro, whatever ya call it, lessons. Whatta ya talkin' about, Joey speaks real good, already!

Kaminski: I think ya just proved my point, Maria. Anyway, the trip'll be a break from the club.

Joey: Yeah, I been meanin' to ask ya about that. I been stuck there for two years singin' the same, old songs. At least, could ya put the comic on ahead of me? I can tell they're already getting' tired of me. Pretty soon they're gonna want me off, so they can see the comic!

Kaminski: You won't be at the Club Rio much longer.

Joey: Why, what's gonna happen?

Kaminski: Somebody wants to buy it.

Joey: Like who? What about your ol' man? When's he gettin' outta the joint? He's gonna wanna go right back to work.

Kaminski: Even if he gets out on good behavior, it's still a helluva long time. I told him that Al Weiss want to buy it and he seemed okay with it. He always hated competin' with Weiss.

Joey: Weiss! Are you jokin'? That gangster? They tried to kill ya, or did ya forget that little detail?

Kaminski: It don't matter. My dad says that if the price is right, sell it. I can still be your manager, ya know.

Joey: That's what worries me.

Maria: I'll let you boys talk. I'm gonna read this article and cut it out and paste it in my scrapbook. [takes newspaper and exits]

Joey: Okay, you do that. *Takes Kaminski aside.* Listen, I wanna ask you somethin'. The War's almost over and when the guys come back home, I think they're gonna be pissed-off at me.

Kaminski: Why would they be pissed-off?

Joey: 'Cause I'm singin' all these sappy songs to their women and they're screamin' and carryin' on.

Kaminski: No, Joey, they'll probly thank ya for keepin' their women warmed up, while they were gone. As far as the sappy, sentimental songs … I think music's gonna change … ya know, happier songs.

Joey: Maybe you're right. But, I gotta tell ya, I think it was last week, when I threw my necktie at some girls in the audience, a coupla of 'em actually threw their panties at me with hotel keys wrapped inside. Thank god, Maria was backstage at the time. I don't know if she's ready for this kinda life.

Kaminski: This life'll get us both nice houses in Long Island. Just you wait and see.

Lights fade to black.

IV, Scene 2

About four days later, Joey Donnetelli and Frank Kaminski are aboard a prop airplane, returning from Los Angeles. The stage is bare, except for what appears to be three airline seats. Joey is seated on the aisle and Kaminski is in the next seat. White overhead spot. The sound effect of a prop plane is loud at first, then diminishes during dialogue.

Stewardess hands Joey a drink and exits.

Kaminski: Isn't that your third?

Joey: Thanks. Without you, I'd lose count. *[Takes gulp, swallows and coughs.]* Listen, Kaminski, I think this whole trip was a waste of time and money.

Kaminski: Whatta ya mean? I mean, what do you mean? You cut a record and you did a screen test.

Joey: So what? They shelved both of them.

Kaminski: Well, that's what they do with new talent. They're just waiting for the right time to release the record. The same thing for the screen test. They're waiting to put you into the right picture.

Joey: The right picture? With all the makeup I was wearing, I could've gotten a part in a Legosi movie! On the bright side, there was a guy at the studio who said that I looked just like Tyrone Power.

Kaminski: That guy was leaning on a broom. He was a janitor! Anyway, Fox doesn't need another Tyrone Power when they've already got one.

Joey: Let's talk about the record. What the hell are they waiting for with that deal?

Kaminski: Okay, let's talk about the record. You didn't do yourself any favors by mocking that Sinatra song, *The House I Live In.* You sang, "The Horse I'm Lovin'."

Joey: Hey, I was just having a good time. The orchestra played along. They were all laughing.

Kaminski: That's a patriotic song, Joey. You're not supposed to do stuff like that! And, if that wasn't enough, you had to sing, "Yank My Doodle, It's a Dandy!" What if they recorded it? You'd be a laughing stock!

Joey: Will you take it easy! You worry too much, Kaminski! It was funnier than hell and you know it! Now, why don't you give me some room and take the window seat?

Kaminski: I don't like window seats on airplanes. I'm afraid of heights.

Joey: Well, don't look out the window!

Kaminski moves to the window seat.

Joey: You know, I just wonder what I'm going to tell Maria … about those things being shelved. Our dreams were tied to my success with those deals.

Kaminski: That's the whole point of doing whatever it takes to be successful. It just takes time, that's all. And if things take off for you, and I think they will, it might be a good idea if we moved to L.A., otherwise we'd be flying back and forth all the time.

Joey: Oh, Maria would never move out of New York. Not as long as her folks are alive and with my luck, they'll both live to be a hundred!

Kaminski: There you go. If you want to let your wife run things ...

Joey: Why don't you just stick to business and leave my wife out of it?

Joey motions for stewardess to get him another drink.

Kaminski: That makes four, Joey.

Joey: It's nowhere near enough, Kaminski. Have you given any thought as to where I'm going to be working, if you sell the club?

An announcement from the Captain interrupts.

Captain: Ahhh, ladies and gentlemen, this is your captain speaking. We've just received some sad news over the radio. President Roosevelt is dead. He was vacationing in Warm Springs, Georgia. Other details are unknown at this time. When I hear more, I'll pass the information on to you. Vice President Truman is now our president. I would like all passengers to join me in a moment of silent prayer. That is all.

Roar of engines increases. Joey and Kaminski stare blankly ahead. Lights fade. Curtain falls.

Act V, Scene 1

The scene opens in a small hotel room. There is an unmade bed in the background. Joey Donnetelli is older, paunchier and has a receding hairline. Joey is seen facing a dresser mirror, dressed in a black tuxedo. He has yet to tie his bowtie. The year is 1958. The place is a casino in Reno, Nevada.

There's a knock at the door. Joey takes off the tux jacket and lays it carefully on the bed. He then opens the door. Frank Kaminski enters, pulls out a chair from in front of a small writing table, positioned almost parallel to the bed and sits. He is dressed in a tailored suit. He also appears to have aged better than Joey. A telephone and a newspaper is on top of the writing desk. There is silence, while Joey returns to the mirror and struggles with his bowtie.

Kaminski: Want me to tie that for you?

Joey: I know how to tie a tie, Kaminski. Do me a large favor and get out!

Kaminski: I just came up to tell you that you're on in half an hour.

Joey: *Gives up trying to tie his bowtie and sits on bed.* I ask for Vegas and you got me some dive in Reno. They didn't even open a big room.

Kaminski: They gave us a small room because I guaranteed a sellout. You know that I was standing out on street corners, handing out playbills to anyone who would take them? I did this yesterday and today.

Joey: *[Sighs.]* Shit, Kaminski, what did I get myself into? I guess things didn't work out as planned, did they?

Kaminski: Well, you could've cooperated a little bit more.

Joey: Oh, like that Broadway audition you sent me to. "It's a lead in a musical," you said. "It's worth a shot," you said. You didn't tell me that they wanted dancers who could sing a little, instead of singers who could dance a little.

Kaminski: Okay, so that was one bum lead. What about the time, I think it was only two years ago, that some of the old-time singers wanted to get together and perform a big show in Chicago. Remember? You refused.

Joey: I told you why. They're a bunch of dried-up, old has-beens. Eddie Cantor and Rudy Vallee, for the luvva Christ! My record, "Let's Give It A Try," sold almost half a million, so how could I be lumped in with those bums?

Kaminski: It was three different versions of the same song, at three different times and it totaled about 340,000. I'm well aware of it. I'm also aware that one of the versions was in Italian. It became very popular at Italian wedding receptions. Music's changing. People are listening to Rock 'n Roll, now. The Big Band Era is over. The ones still working, have dwindled down to five-piece combos.

Joey: What the hell do you want me to do, start singing *Hound Dog*, or something? *[Stands and starts singing a swing version, with an extra beat.]* "You ain't nothin' but a hound dog, cryin' all of the time." *[Sits back on the bed.]* All I know is the standards and I'll keep singing them as long as people want to hear them.

Kaminski: The only ones who want to hear that stuff are blue-haired old ladies and their bald-headed husbands. And, another thing, nobody's going to swoon or throw their panties at you, anymore. The girls are screaming for Elvis, not Joey Donnetelli. You have to adapt to what's popular! And for the love of god, stop doing those joke lyrics. You're booked for three more nights, so please, please don't sing, Onward Christian Soldiers Marching On a Whore. It's not nice!

Joey: You want nice? Go work for Perry Como. Now, will you vacate the premises? In other words, don't let the door hitcha where the good lord splitcha.

[Kaminski exits. Joey puts the jacket on and, returning to the mirror, attempts to tie the bowtie, again.

Joey: Oh, the hell with it. It's coming off, anyway. [turns off room light and exits. Stage goes black, then transforms into a performance stage. Amber spot is on Joey. Joey has a hand mic. He whips cord]

Joey: *[To unseen band.]* Maestro, if you will. *[Band begins playing, Let's Give It A Try, up-tempo, as Joey syncopates.]* "If you are so inclined, my love, and if the stars that're above, say it is right for us, [light applause, muffled laughter. Then, let us give it a try, just you and I. Under the stars above, I will pledge you my love. Let our hearts soar into love. Let us give it a try, just you and I ... just you and I."

Joey throws his bowtie into the audience. Laughter becomes louder. Spotlight focuses to pinpoint, then fades. Sounds fade to echo.

V, Scene 2

Lights come up to reveal the hotel room, again. Joey enters with a towel around his neck, takes off his jacket and throws it on the bed, which is now made-up. He walks over to the writing table, sits and picks up the phone. There's a knock at the door. With an air of weary disgust, he gets up and opens the door. It's a bellhop with a bottle of champagne in an ice bucket and two glasses.

Bellhop: Compliments of the management, Mr. Donnetelli.

Joey: Two glasses? Do you see anybody else in the room, genius? *[Puts bottle on writing desk and pulls a dollar bill from his pocket.]* Here's a buck for all your trouble. *[Bellhop exits, Joey goes back to the phone.]* Operator? Yes, I want to place a long-distance call, collect, to Gramercy 6-9130. Queens, New York. *[Pause.]* Maria? Hi, it's me. It's pretty awful. That goddam Kaminski doesn't know what he's doing. Three more nights. Two shows on Saturday and Sunday. I know it's something, but there's nothing for me when I get back, except the usual joints in the city and a couple in Jersey, for chrisakes! Well, I can't! Kaminski's got me half nuts! People hate me, here. Probably because they don't like my music. I'm never coming back to Reno, that's for sure! How's your folks? I knew it. They'll probably outlive me, at the rate I'm going. Is little Joey around? Oh, I forgot you're three hours later. Tell him that when I come home, I'll take him to see the Yankees. See that's another thing, Maria. First, the Giants move, then the Dodgers. California's got everything! They don't need baseball too. I think the whole world's gone nuts! Okay, okay. This is costing money. I'll try to take the first flight out on Monday. Love you. Goodbye.

Joey gets up and towels off his face and throws towel on bed. There's a knock at the door.

Kaminski: It's me. Let me in. I've got some terrific news for you.

Joey: What do you want, now? *[returns to the chair and sits]* Kaminski, open the bottle and take a snort. I want to talk to you.

Kaminski: First, the good news. A call came in at the front desk. It was Disney Studios. They're auditioning for voice-overs ...

Joey: [interrupting] For some stupid cartoon?

Kaminski: Well, yes. That's some of what they do over there.

Joey: Okay, I'll think about it. *[Short pause.]* Time's up. The answer's no. I'm paying you twenty per cent to find me some decent work and all you do is goof around.

Kaminski: Twenty per cent of nothing is nothing. If you were my only client, I'd starve to death.

Joey: Who are your other clients? Oh, I forgot. A hokey magician and a comic, left-over from vaudeville who don't, doesn't, have any teeth ... can't even afford 'em!

Kaminski: Sometimes I spend my own money to promote you, Joey.

Joey: Well, why don't you stop doing it?

Kaminski: What do you mean by that?

Joey: What I mean, Kaminski, is that you're fired. I'm going to find somebody else. *[Joey dials the phone, while watching Kaminski.]* Operator? Get me the William Morris Agency in Los Angeles.

Kaminski walks behind Joey, glares at him, then crosses toward the door and exits.

Joey: *[Reaches a receptionist at the agency.]* Hi, could I speak to one of your agents? *[Pauses.]* Tell him it's Joey Donnetelli ... Joey ...

Donnetelli … You know, Joey Donnetelli! Wait, don't hang up! *[Joey holds the phone in front of his face and stares at the receiver for a few seconds, then rises with the receiver in his hand and starts walking toward the door. He turns back and hangs up the phone. He continues walking toward the door.]*

Joey: Kaminski, get back here! *[Opens door.]* Kaminski! *[Steps outside the door, out of sight.]* Kaminski! *[Comes back into room and walks to a suitcase which is lying on the bed. Joey is in profile, as he opens suitcase. He reaches in and pulls out a small revolver. Then, turns to audience. Opens the cylinder, examines it, flips the cylinder shut and places the gun back into the suitcase. He returns to the writing table and sits. The chair is facing the audience. He leans back. His arms hang down at his sides. Overhead spot tightens on Joey's face. The phone rings. He glances at the phone on the third ring, then turns away. Spot fades, as phone continues to ring. Curtain falls as phone ringing also fades.]*

The End

The Camp

After having been summoned to the Director's office, I had the opportunity to actually admire the symmetry of rows and rows of olive-drab, two-story barracks, which were fanned out in a perfect semi-circle. In the center, was the office of the Director, also a two-story building; main level office with living quarters upstairs. And the same color as the rest of the barracks.

In all the years I've been here, it was only the second time I'd met with the Director. The first was probably a welcoming meeting. This one was for reasons so far, unknown. This time, I had nothing but questions and I'm sure that the Director's heard the same questions many times and already had the answers.

I cautiously approached the secretary's desk. "I'm here to see the Director. I've got an appointment."

"Have a seat."

She was an older woman, perhaps the Director's wife.

After waiting about five minutes, she announced, "The Director will see you, now. Go right in."

Seated behind an antique, mahogany desk in a high-backed swivel chair, the Director stared, not at me, but at some papers on his desk. He took off his reading glasses and lifted his ice-blue eyes in my direction, but still not looking directly at me. Placing his hands, palms down on the desk top, he leaned forward. I leaned back. Curiously, he opened a desk drawer.

"Would you like to know why I've asked you here? Uh, Mr. Jackson?"

"I'm honored, sir. But, why?"

"I've decided to increase your security level to ten. Which means that you can walk through camp, anywhere you want, unescorted."

"Thank you. I appreciate that, sir."

"As you know, Mr. Jackson, your parents haven't achieved the high level of clearance which you have. And I think you know why. They'd been known as highly subversive before they entered the camp and I understand they continue to be subversive *within* the camp. Your father was brought to the attention of the Intelligence Services by his

147

co-workers. He was fired for making incendiary remarks about the president. Your mother, as subversive as anyone, was a video news commentator on social media, who continually made similar statements."

"What can I do about it, Director?"

"I can't think of anything you can personally do, except to keep resisting their attempts to indoctrinate you to their way of thinking. And I think you've done remarkably well, Mr. Jackson, at doing that. Let's see, you're currently at Level Ten. At Level Fifteen, you're eligible to be released from camp to rejoin society."

"I've got a question, Director. Why were we, as American citizens, put in camps? This has happened before, hasn't it?"

"Yes, but it was a long time ago. And it was for national security. We feared they would be loyal to their country of national origin. Besides, it was for their own protection, as well."

"Another question, Director; the military coup which took over the federal government, was ten years ago. So, why are we still here?"

"There are hundreds of these camps throughout the southwest part of the country. I am the Director of only this camp and report to the government everything that happens in *this* camp. The other Directors do the same thing with their camps. When *all* the camps are in compliance with federal re-education requirements *and* all have achieved Level Fifteen clearance, we will set the internees free to join the new order, at approximately the same time. Of course, older people are set in their ways and it's harder to convince them to accept the future. They don't seem to realize that it's for their own good."

I could barely stand to listen to the same bullshit coming from the Director and his goons. Here I am, thirty-two years old, living in a single room with my parents and sitting in re-education classes with them. While I was able to act like I was absorbing the brainwashing, I understand how difficult it was for people like my parents.

The constant surveillance by the black-uniformed, private police force; the electrified fence, the transponders, surgically implanted, upon arrival, in everyone's arms, our faded blue clothing were becoming just part of our daily lives. Unfortunately, those who accepted this controlled environment, couldn't see the harm it was doing.

We were taken care of, though. The barracks were air-conditioned, the food was good, we weren't treated badly, our medical needs were attended to, but this only leads to false feelings of well-being, followed by complacency.

There was no contact with the outside world, except for the weekly newsletter from the Director. Of course, it was highly propagandized, mostly lies and often repeated about how the government was making "great strides" to improve the lives of its citizens.

It was shortly after the coup, that all nationwide elections were abolished, habeas corpus was suspended indefinitely, and martial law was established. Hundreds, perhaps thousands of Americans were transferred to camps. In our camp, alone, there were seven-hundred of us.

"And I'm going to admonish you for one thing, Mr. Jackson. May I call you, Robert?"

"Yes."

"While it's not exactly forbidden, it *is* discouraged to socially mix with races other than your own. Now, I understand that you've chosen a white girlfriend. Aren't there enough black females from which to choose? What is her name? It's Rose, isn't it? What a quaint name.

This made me want to leap across the desk and choke the son-of-a-bitch, but I was mindful of the open desk drawer and what kind of weapon may lie inside.

"The woman ... Susan, whom I was dating and someday hoped to marry, is in a camp in Nevada. I'm stuck here in the Mojave Desert and can't even communicate with her."

"Now, now, don't worry. Maybe you'll see her again, sooner than you think."

"Yeah, *maybe.*"

A surprised look momentarily crossed his face. He stood and we shook hands. The conversation was over.

Walking back to the barracks, I kept thinking about the fact that escape was on everyone's mind, but how? How could we possibly overtake the armed, ubiquitous guards? We couldn't effectively accomplish this unless we had the same plan. This was next to impossible, since we weren't allowed to communicate with other internees. Even within our own barrack's, congregate dining hall, we couldn't talk, or whisper to each other. But, outside, one-on-one, we could. As long as it was normal conversations, not hatching some escape plan.

Other than the electrified fence, the biggest obstacle to escaping, were the transponders. If there actually was anyplace to go, they would've found us in a matter of minutes.

My parents and I had finished the daily work detail; carrying six bags of garbage out of our barracks to the dumpster. It was also an opportunity to visit Rose outside of her barracks.

When I first met Rose, she had long, blond hair. But, in the camp's successful effort to humiliate and control us, both physically and psychologically, the males were given buzz-cuts every week and the females, had their hair cropped to their jawlines. So, after a few weeks, Rose's hair turned from blond to brunette.

"The guards are watching us."

"I know, aren't they always?"

Rose laughed, "They've got it in their heads that we're trouble makers."

"That's the truth, according to them. Then again, perhaps we are."

She turned her back to the guard and faced me. "There are people, singles and couples who're younger than us. But, we don't see children anywhere. There *has* to be some."

I pretended to scratch my nose so I could cover my mouth. "Do you suppose that pregnant women were given abortions?"

"No, I think the children became wards of the state ... put in orphanages."

Again, I covered my mouth. "That makes sense. Young minds are more easily indoctrinated ... more malleable."

"Robert, do you think there are spies planted among us, who report to the Director, everyone's activities?"

"I don't doubt it for a second. Here comes a guard. Act like I've said something funny and laugh. Just don't overdo it."

"What're you two talking about?"

"The weather," Rose answered, "it sure is hot today. And you must be broiling in that black uniform."

"That's *my* problem," said the guard. "If you think it's so hot, why don't *you* go inside?"

I told Rose that I'd see her later and said goodbye.

Earlier, she'd told me that she was here with her mother and they both had advanced to Level Eight clearance. Her father, a university Humanities professor, had been arrested and executed as part of the government's purge of rebellious intellectuals during the onset of the war.

Rose and I had been friends since day-two of our incarceration. We enjoyed each other's company, but we were forbidden any intimate contact. We shared an occasional kiss, done quickly in the few seconds of serendipitous privacy.

We met again two days later and Rose explained that the Director had promoted her and her mother to Level Ten.

"You skipped over Level Nine?"

"Yes. I'm just as surprised as *you* are."

"I don't know how you did it, but congratulations. Now we're able to meet anytime, anyplace, not just at your barracks."

She smiled when I said that. But, there was something different. Her eyes seemed to belie that smile. Was it only my imagination? I shrugged the thought away.

"At Level Fifteen, when we're freed," I asked, "would they remove the transponders from our bodies?"

"I'm not sure, but you'd think so. What would be the point in continuing to track us?"

"That's what I'm afraid of. There might *be* a purpose. Who the hell knows?"

The following year, late afternoon, in June, the camp's warning sirens began to howl. An earthquake had struck the camp. I managed to get my frightened parents out of our cheaply built barracks before it collapsed. We ran from the thirty-foot gash which crossed west to east, through the camp. Other barracks collapsed and some fell into the fissure along with a portion of the goddam electrified fence. I assumed that it had short-circuited the entire fence.

After I made certain that my parents were safe and less terrified, I rushed to Rose's barracks. It also had collapsed into rubble. I was relieved to see Rose and her mother standing nearby, their jaws slackened.

"I'm happy to see that you're both okay!"

"We are. Just a little shaken."

"Will you look at the guards running around aimlessly? I hope they all fall into the hole!"

My comment elicited only a smirk from Rose.

Her mother was about my parents' age, but looked more worn and haggard. Maybe that's because age shows up more in white people. Rose had told me she was three years older than I was, but looked older than that.

The camp's power was out and it was starting to get dark and soon, the only light would be from the guards' flashlights and the light of a half-moon.

"All right," one of the guards bellowed through a bullhorn, "the Director has an announcement to make. Stay where you are."

"Thank god, he's okay," I whispered to Rose.

She poked me in the ribs with her elbow and shushed me, trying not to grin.

The guard handed the bullhorn to the Director: "Most of our barracks have been destroyed and ten of you have lost their lives. I'm truly sorry for that.

"In addition, I've received word that the government will be closing this camp. You will be transferred to other nearby camps. Of course, we'll try to keep families together."

What if my parents and I were transferred to the camp in Nevada? I immediately thought of a reunion with Susan, but what about Rose? Even though I enjoyed Rose's companionship over the years, it still seemed temporary. I couldn't help wanting to be with Susan more than anyone else.

"Rose, I'm going over to where I left my parents and bring them over here with us."

A couple of hours later, an unfamiliar rumbling was heard and moving closer. Initially, I thought it was an aftershock. This alerted the guards, as they began to spread out. A huge armored truck, with its lights off, crashed through the fence, followed by another and another. A half-dozen men jumped out from each vehicle. They were heavily armed and wearing military combat gear. They were also wearing night-vision goggles.

The guards immediately raised their weapons. The guard, who was standing nearest me, was shot by one of the invaders. I told people standing with us to get down.

I glanced at the dead guard and shivered when I saw the enormous exit wound in his back. Were they using some kind of exploding ammunition?

Other guards fell, mortally wounded. It looked as if everyone wearing black was being shot. The shooting continued for several minutes, until another vehicle slammed through the fence. Then, the shooting began once more.

A man, whom I guessed was their leader, spoke through a bullhorn.

"I think it's time for an explanation as to what's happening here. We are a militia group."

Echoes, in the distance from two other bullhorns were repeating what was being said to our small group.

"Don't be afraid. We're on your side and we're going to get you out of here. We were nearby, waiting for the right opportunity to liberate this camp. This is our first of many more.

"The federal government's been restored. Due process is back in place. The president's been deposed, arrested and jailed. Did I hear somebody ask, 'What about the vice president?' There is no vice president, right now. The president had given himself absolute power, completing his wish to become a dictator."

Mutterings rose from the crowd, becoming louder. The militia man raised his hand to silence us.

"We have commandeered a passenger train to transport all of you to Los Angeles area hospitals for removal of your transponders. Those of you without transponders, will be suspected as government collaborators, working as spies in this camp."

Rose and I suspected as much. I drew her closer to me.

"Line up single file," the man ordered, "we'll begin scanning all of you for transponders."

Several of the militia spread throughout the camp with their scanners.

After they were scanned, people stood out of line and watched as others were scanned. Then, they came to Rose and her mother. One of the militia men started leading them away to join a small group.

"Rose, what're you doing?" I yelled, "don't go with him!"

I tried to intervene but was pushed and told to step back. Did it mean that they didn't have transponders? What was going to happen to them? Rose looked back. It was the saddest look I'd ever seen from her. Her shoulders slumped, as she looked away.

I learned that following the scanning process, it turned out there were about twenty spies, camp-wide.

Suddenly, we heard a lone gunshot coming from the Director's residence. Any assumptions of what had happened, were proven correct.

It's been three years since we were freed. I gave up trying to find Rose, if only to ask her why she was recruited as a camp spy. Likewise, I also gave up trying to find Susan and as time went by, my thoughts of both had diminished.

The *new* government repeatedly apologized for the "inconvenience" we'd suffered for twelve years of imprisonment and we were promised a small amount of money to help us begin a new life ... a payment which has yet to be delivered.

My parents and I are presently renting a modest bungalow in Anaheim and when Disneyland re-opened, we took part-time jobs there.

We learned that our former president was tried, convicted of treason and exiled to Tijuana.

Welcome Home

All hell broke loose on that hot, steamy, August night, in 1945. Some of them were certain that an invasion of Okinawa was imminent. Tracer artillery fire from the battleships in the North China Sea and the Pacific, thundered and lit the sky. On the horizon, the faint silhouette of the U.S.S. Missouri could be seen during intermittent flashes, cannons roaring.

Dave Anderson grabbed his helmet and rifle and dove for cover. Others did the same. One guy had a shovel and was feverishly digging a foxhole. *There isn't time,* Dave thought, *this is it! Damn Kamikazes!* Then, he could hear some guys shouting nearby, followed by the stutter of automatic rifles.

An officer ran by yelling, "What're you doing, you morons? The war's over! It's over! Japan surrendered!" Dave rolled onto his back and laughed.

He had been sent to Ie Shima, Okinawa in June, with the 77th Infantry Division and had learned that two months earlier, famed war-correspondent, Ernie Pyle, had been killed by a sniper.

It wasn't until December that Dave got his separation orders which read that he was to be, at the "convenience of the government, demobilized." It was standard military jargon meaning, discharge.

Late in December, he boarded a transport ship and headed for San Francisco. From there, he got on a train bound for the separation center, Camp McCoy, Wisconsin. Another soldier, who was also going there, told Dave that the camp had been used to house German and Japanese POW's and wondered if some of them were still there.

Dave spent most of his time re-reading some of his wife, Sarah's letters. In one, she wrote that she'd rented out a spare room to a young man named Frank. In another, she said the company for which Dave worked, *Swanson Ice and Coal,* had gone out of business because people began buying refrigerators and getting their furnaces refitted for natural gas. She went on to say that it might be easy for a returning G.I. to get a job. Men, who didn't have to go into the service, were earning a hundred dollars a week! That's what her tenant, Frank was making. *Nobody's worth a hundred dollars a week,* he thought. Her last letter stated that she and their son, Mike, would drive to McCoy to pick him up.

It was toward the middle of January, 1946, that Dave arrived at McCoy. He underestimated the time it took to muster out, so Sarah and Mike had to stay overnight in Sparta.

After breakfast in the mess hall, he was free to leave. Free to finally go home.

When he saw his wife and son, he let his duffle bag slide off his shoulder. Sarah had coached Mike to run and give his daddy a hug. Dave dropped to one knee and hugged his son.

"You're such a big boy! Gee, you grew up fast!" tears welled-up, "How old are you, now?"

"Four and a half."

Sarah walked toward him with arms outstretched, "Welcome home, honey!" They embraced and kissed long enough to make Mike tug at his mother's skirt.

"Okay, then. Let's go home."

They chatted as they drove, with Sarah driving, Dave sitting beside her and Mike in the back seat.

About a mile out, Mike interrupted his parents, "Daddy's home, now. Does that mean that Uncle Frank has to move out?"

Sarah quickly jerked her head toward Mike and gave him a withering glance, which meant from previous experiences, for him to shut up. She turned back and looked straight ahead, expressionless, except that she was blushing.

"Uncle Frank, Sarah? Uncle Frank?"

There was silence for the next one-hundred-seventy miles and after that, more silence.

The Envelope

A few years ago, I received a letter in the mail. It was a plain, white envelope, addressed to me, with no return address. An acquaintance warned me not to open such an envelope because of a nationwide fear that it may contain "amtrax."

Acknowledging his malapropism, I laughed and said, "Why would anyone be afraid of passenger trains?"

"What? No, you idiot! *Amtrax*! It's a poison! On the other hand, go ahead and open it. See if I care."

"Can I come over to your house and open it?"

"No! You are one crazy motherfucker! You know that?"

"I know that *you* think so."

Deciding to take the proper precautions, I brought the envelope to the nearest police station. I gave no explanation to the desk clerk, instead asked to see an officer.

"We're kinda busy, today. Do you have something you wanted to give him? Otherwise, it's gonna be a long wait."

"Yes, this envelope." I slid it through a slot under the bulletproof window.

Later that evening, while watching the local *News at Six*, I was shocked to hear the announcement:

"Sixty-three-year old, police department clerk, Florence Jorgenson, was found dead at her desk today. Apparently, she had opened a suspicious-looking envelope possibly containing the nerve agent, amtra ... excuse me, *anthrax*. Police are combing the area looking for possible suspects."

I gasped, clapping a hand to my mouth.

The anchor man was handed a piece of paper. "This just in: The envelope in question did *not* contain anthrax. I repeat, did *not*. Rather, it contained baking powder. Mrs. Jorgenson did not die from exposure to the substance."

I laughed in relief and said to myself, *you figured that out yourself, huh genius?*

I tuned in later for *News at Ten* and checked for developments since six o'clock.

They had a taped interview with Lieutenant Herm Gutkneckt of the Third Precinct: "We consider this a copycat crime. Yeah, it's *still* a serious crime and we're going to find the son-of-a-(bleep) what did this. Unfortunately, the only witness to the suspect's identity, is dead."

Well, case closed as far as I was concerned, but I felt bad about poor Mrs. Jorgenson. She might've been scared to death when she saw the powder and thought it was anthrax.

Freelancer

I'd worked my way through college doing minor freelance work for local publications. But then, decided to broaden my scope by interviewing people who once made important contributions, but are now, largely forgotten.

My plan was to find some of these people, interview them and sell the material to the highest bidder.

I found one such individual on the internet; a former jazz saxophonist, named Luther Briggs, living in a Chicago nursing home. He was eighty-eight years old. He'd abruptly stopped performing at the age of twenty. What the hell?

Intrigued, I phoned him, he agreed to an interview and told me the address of the home. I packed a camera and recorder and drove four-hundred miles to meet with him.

At first, I thought the home would be a nasty-smelling place. To my surprise, it was a rather pleasant, welcoming environment. I found him in his room, sitting in a chair. His eyes were alert and bright. I walked over and shook his left hand, noticing that his right hand was a prosthetic. I'd ask him about that, later.

Clicking on the recorder, I decided to do a Q and A type of format.

Q: I'm very glad to meet you, Mr. Briggs. Are you ready to begin?

A: *Mr.* Briggs? Forget that. Call me Loody. People useta call me that.

Q: Okay, Loody, what type of saxophone did you play?

A: E-flat alto. Started playing when I was sixteen in the late 1940s.

Q: The big band era?

A: It was toward the end of the big bands. They already were startin' to break-up into smaller combos. I played with some well-known big bands, though.

Q: What were some of them?

A: Lemme see. There was Dorsey, Miller, Goodman, Shaw. After that, I got a job at Capitol Records with the house band. Everybody who was anybody, did recordin' sessions there. One day, Sinatra walks in … a real pain in the ass. Everythin' *hadda* be perfect. Those were some long days and nights, man. He's the one who first called me a *sex* player an' the name stuck.

Q: Sex player?

A: Yeah, he was jokin', a'course, but he said that I made my horn sound like a woman havin' sex. Sounds like, gigglin' and low, sexy moans. And he said that he never heard anything like it, before.

Q: That's quite a gift!

A: Yeah, I used it as often as I could. On the blues numbers, I could make my horn sound like it was cryin'.

Q: So, you can be heard on dozens of records?

A: Damned straight! A lotta solo stuff, too.

Q: What happened? Why did you stop playing?

A: I tried to enroll at Julliard, but they said they couldn't accept grade school dropouts ... some shit like that. So, I stayed in New York for a while, ya know, ta rub shoulders with some of the greats. I even went ta Paris ta study and worked some gigs ta pay my rent. Then, it happened. I got my draft notice ... flew ta Jersey an' was inducted inta the Army infantry. I was only nineteen. How 'bout that? They sent me direct to fuckin' Korea!

Q: Is that where you hurt your hand?

A: *Hurt* it? That's where I lost it! Some North Korean bastard shot me in the hand. I don't know if the Doc's even *tried* to fix it ... man, they just lopped it off.

Q: They amputated it?

A: That's what I said. The good news is that they sent me home. Ever try to play a sax left handed? Ya need *both* hands. I was washed-up in the music biz.

Q: Well, did you try using a different instrument? Or, is that a foolish question.

A: The only other instrument I could play was the clarinet. That's not gonna work either, with only one fuckin' hand.

Q: What did you wind up doing after you were discharged?

A: I went ta work at a music store an' taught young kids how ta play their instruments.

Q: Then, they learned from a master craftsman.

A: That's right. Summa those kids turned out ta be pretty good.

Q: Did any of them turn professional?

A: I don't know, but I'm sure summa them did.

Q: I think I've got what I needed here. Is there anything more you wanted to add?

A: Nope. Wait a minute, there *is* one more thing; I hadda nurse help me draw up a contract between me an' you. It says that when ya sell this, I get half of what ya make.

Q: What? That's outrageous!

A: Well, if you don't sign it, I'm gonna sell my story, myself, ta anybody who wants ta buy it.

I'd be stupid to walk away without his permission, so I tried to negotiate. I offered forty percent to him and sixty percent for myself. He countered with the reverse equation. I caved-in and accepted.

I sent out copies to some periodicals, to no avail. Some unknown writer heard about it and I sold him the rights for a hundred dollars. Better than nothing, I thought, and sent a sixty-dollar check to Loody.

It turned out that the guy who bought it, was a screenwriter. He, in turn, sold it to some rinky-dink movie producer and it wound up on pay-per-view. I paid six bucks to see it. It wasn't very good. In fact, it stunk! I still feel that *I* could've done a better job. That was ten years ago and I'm *still* kicking myself in the ass!

Acknowledgements

"Freedom Rider" was previously published as a memoir in *Whistling Shade Literary Journal, Spring-Summer, 2013.*

"The Photograph" was previously published in *The Ramingo's Porch, Issue 2, Spring 2018.*

About the author

J.P. Johnson is a retired real estate agent from Northeast Minneapolis. Retirement allows him more time for writing, which is his passion. J.P. Johnson is the author of a previous collection, *Convoluted Tales*.

Lost Lake Folk Art
SHIPWRECKT BOOKS PUBLISHING COMPANY

IN®
DIE

Minnesota

Made in the USA
Columbia, SC
09 September 2018